ABOUT THE AUTHOR

THOMAS S. JOHNSON (1987 -) was born in Houston, Texas to a middle-class family, and raised in a small town in East Texas. Johnson graduated from the University of Texas at Austin with a Bachelor of Journalism and a Bachelor of Science in Radio-Television Film, before working as a reporter in both print and broadcast news. He later enlisted in the United States Army in hopes of paying off his education, and mostly achieved this goal. He married his wife while stationed overseas and left the Army after serving five years. They live in Austin, Texas with their dog, Finch. This is his first publication.

Matt -

these were some of the greatest times and I'll never forget them all. But!

the adventure never ends and I wish you the best on them all! You'll remain an inspiration always.

Tom Johnson
Oct 17

THINGS I'VE NEVER DONE

Collected Work, 2011 – 2015

T. S. Johnson

Published by T. S. Johnson

Published by T. S. Johnson, 2017
T. S. Johnson (USA), Austin, Texas 78751, U.S.A.

Cover designs and photography by T. S. Johnson

Printed in the United States of America

For inquiries, contact tomjohnson@utexas.edu.

We all have this power.

Prologue

The following selections are a near entire collection of everything my mind had the strength to say during the days between the years of 2011 to 2015. It is exhaustive, more in its production than its compilation. I have chosen, in spite of the better argument, to leave them in chronological order. You will find them of all sorts in a row: poetry, prose, non-fiction, autobiographical fiction, etc. My hopes are sincere that by suffering their logical chronology something from their illogical cohesion will come to the surface. There is little satisfaction trying to describe why in the moments of creation I felt compelled to write this way or that, but, here they are in their respective forms.

Part I consists of the earliest months I spent in the United States Army training as a soldier before leaving the continent. An addendum included here is comprised of *Howling Like Animals with Fangs to the Moon,* an intended collection composed during this time and published here the same. *Part II* consists of the years I spent abroad, first in Europe, later in the Middle East, and once again back in Europe. With *Part III*, I finally returned to the states and exited the Army. The writings will reflect these movements clearly, reflexively.

The things inside can be vulgar, obscene, and even offensive, but underneath is the truth as I saw it during these years. The words contained here will tell you all you need to know.

Part I

FORMING UP

January 2011 – October 2011

The Gross Monotony of It All

The gross monotony of it all caught me quite by surprise the other night, and not for the best of reasons. Less than 48 hours out from my ship date to the United States Army, I found, as previously thought, that the best way for me to spend my final hours would be with those I knew and love best: my friends in Austin, the ones with whom I spent my formative years and the ones for whom I owe most of my life. As it were, everything went according to plan aside from the rain and for their presence at my going-away party I cannot thank these friends enough. In no small way I learned clearly that the ones who care about the direction of my life were there; sadly, many that I thought were in that group were not present. That of course is a discussion for another time.

The party, however, started early and went late into the night. A typical person of post-collegiate age living in Austin would love it and fit right in. But there I was – somewhere around midnight, tossing plastic ping pong balls into plastic cups in a competitive manner, laughing, drinking, having fun, or so they say. In that moment, though, I realized just exactly what we're all missing: that each moment of our life is an exact indictment of who we are...

...And for all you who are lonely, sad, lost, depressed, or searching, I ask then why you continue to behave in a way that does not achieve the ends you seek?

I see all around me people in their late twenties (an age appropriately determined through social and religious mores to establish our future identity) drinking, carousing, and in no way accomplishing or behaving in any way that would achieve their goals. Now, I for one do not necessarily agree with marriage, relationships, and jobs as they currently exist or even believe that these things are worth our time and expense, but that's not important to the point. The people who do believe in marriage, relationships, and jobs are still drinking, still carousing, and still not doing anything to achieve those ends.

If you are lonely, why then do you continue to go downtown looking for a one-night stand, something surely anyone would agree could not lead to a lasting relationship?

If you are sad, why then do you continue to stay indoors whittling away the hours watching television and not spent outside where you could fulfill yourself physically and conceivably make friends?

If you are discontent, why then do you continue to work at a dead-end job where you hate your boss, despise your coworkers, and go home to get drunk due to stress?

The most salient point I learned this past spring while in the company of a woman, who in her late twenties was serving tables at a steakhouse and skipping classes she was enrolled in, would answer the question "What's next?" with "something will come along." I'd bet money that everyone has heard the phrase "something will come along" more times than we can bear and don't even think of its significance or its literal meaning anymore. Frankly, it's offensive – to think that something will just "come along" implies that good things are always ahead, and it removes from blame the most important facet of this world: *we have only ourselves to motivate and blame for every action, circumstance, and consequence, good or bad.*

If you don't like your job, *get a new one now.*
If you aren't happy in your relationship, *get out now.*
If you aren't making good grades, *start studying now.*
If you don't like your surroundings, *move away now.*

The sheer notion that we aren't responsible for our circumstances is despicable. Action is the only true way to improvement because experience is the only way to wisdom, and experience is bore through activity. Do not watch your life pass before you do exactly what you want, be it any of the things

I have mentioned.

For myself, it was joining the Army. The Army itself was not my immediate and most front goal – changing who I was in a drastic and violent way, was. I was broke – unemployed. I was lonely – sleeping around. I was tired – stuck in a rut. And I was not proud of who I was – the Army would make a man out of me. To reinforce these points, I must illustrate that we cannot find a fix-all.

I visited a good friend of mine in Phoenix last week. It was for all intents and purposes a great thrill to see her again. But what touched me most was that both she and her boyfriend were, in the six months since my enlistment, the first persons to ask me the question that I was avoiding myself: How could I possibly give my life to a cause I cannot support? That's to say, how can I become a weapon of death in a war of oppression? The answer is in no way simple, and I point most notably to Book I of Plato's *The Republic*. In it, Socrates has a dialogue with Polemarchus about the nature and structure of justice, and its uses when applied to both the individual and the individual's country. Here, the most important question is, should one serve himself through pursuing the mind or should one strengthen his soul through service to country? And though I cannot contrive a singular answer to the question, my service in the Army will attain both goals – by serving the country, I am serving myself. So back to the question posed by my friends: how could I give my life to a cause I cannot support? Because I was disgusted with myself. Plain and simple. I haven't been as happy as I am since enlisting in a long, long time. And without going into expansive detail, the argument here comes full circle – I wasn't happy, so I changed myself violently and forever.

So I leave with this implicit directive: *do something violent in your life to achieve any goal.* Without violent and immediate change, we cannot expect anything to improve or worsen, and surely cannot spend our time waiting for "something to come along." The time of our life is not a period of years, but each minute that we're alive. Do not spend the entirety of your life attempting to recreate certain moments.

If you want love, go and make love.
If you want money, start working with vicious zeal.
If you want happiness, start reading more.
If you want success, practice your craft without abandon.

It is only through our actions that any end, better or worse, can be possessed. Because if you don't use caution, the gross monotony of it all will consume you.

There Are People Who Care, Pt. I

There are people who care. They may not know why they care, what it means for them to care, or *even know that they care at all*, but they do exist. Do not let the light of your hope go out before you find these people. It takes a search sometimes, or other times they walk right up and ask for a cigarette.

The latter happened to me late Sunday night in Adams-Morgan, a suburb of the District of Columbia area. I had been visiting the Capitol for a few days on my pass from the base and found no better way to spend my weekend than walking the steps of our great political cathedrals. On this particular night though we had made our way to Adams-Morgan for our second visit, having decided through exhaustive exploration that the area was our best chance for a good drinkin' time. Surprisingly in fact, D.C. has not much in the way of good drinking districts, or so we could find, yet this one area on the northeast side of town had something in the way of Austin's Sixth Street. Every bit as quirky too.

A cousin of mine had suggested a place called Madam's Organ, which doesn't take much to decipher is an entendre of the locale. I didn't even get in the door before I heard a band covering "How's About You", and a wonderful rendition of the Rolling Stones' "Dead Flowers" would follow. When combined with the spectral atmosphere of red Christmas lights, nude paintings, random taxidermy, and stairs so canted you'd feel like falling, it was all I could do to contain my joy. The band consisted of five members, Sarah & the Tall Boys they were, each a master of their craft. The pedal steel cried throughout the walls and it goes without any surprise to say that I spent much of the time dancing with the women in the bar, and having a good time of it.

What saddened me during all of this was the people's inability to dance. I can't find a better way to say it, because I don't want to knock on anyone who's at least moving their feet to the music, but there was no indication that anyone in the D.C. area had any idea how to dance. What was most shameful was that, when halfway through a tune and tired of stepping on feet, they would often resort to just jumping around. There's a time and a place for that, but during Merle Haggard's "I'll Just Sit Here and Drink," one need not jump straight up. There was one moment where, rather than bounce around obnoxiously, the person next to me decided to do his best Texan impression by grabbing the invisible belt buckle and cowboy hat and proceed to kick around. I let him know that I was offended (kidding of course), but the most amazing thing happened next. The cute pint-sized female that was with this group immediately seized the opportunity to introduce herself, ask me the proper way to dance, and proceed to show her. Her excitement glowed on her face when she went to ask me what I was doing in town, when I had moved there, and when I could take her and her friends line dancing, all before I could answer a single question. So, when I did answer and explained that I was visiting, didn't live there, and was in the military, she deflated immediately. There was a literal washing away of her smile and it seemed as if the conversation was dead thereto. I am not saddened by any of this, but use it as an illustration of the way things may come to be for me for some time now, and wish her only the best as she attempts to learn to dance. "Quick-quick-slow," was all I told her to remember, and I pray she does. Maybe some good came from that encounter after all.

The reverse of this happenstance is the one I alluded to in the introduction of this article. The night went long as the band played three sets, each time broken up by cigarettes outside where I learned the band members were from Chicago, had been traveling south and eastward, and were delighted to know that someone in the D.C. area could pick out the songs from their repertoire. During that conversation we both expressed our bewilderment that just above the wonderful bars and chandeliers of Madam's Organ's first floor was a dance floor and DJ where the typical scene was set: dance floor, men and women fabricating attractions, and alcohol all around. As it would turn out, this would become the longest lasting scene in the night and that's where I would stay, if only to meet more people. And one came along.

I didn't even get her name.

It was after the bar closed as I stood outside the front door at 3am, not even holding a grin, when up walked the most beautiful girl who asked me for a cigarette. I didn't have any out so it could of been my aura or her need for a smoke that drove the connection. Whatever it was, I supplied her request and we went on to share a cigarette. What was best was the conversation we shared too. She was a teacher of 7th grade English, a lower-class school where the children were underprivileged. It didn't take more than two questions to learn that she was passionately upset that children there had no desire to engage their minds and that by the time anyone reaches college, if they get there, they have no inclination toward a liberal education that teaches one to be a human being, much less a trained professional. Of course you don't have to look any further here to see that it lit me up like a whorehouse to hear these words. We were shortly interrupted and she left to meet her roommate before I could finish the conversation. It was here that I saw her walking away and couldn't help but run up again.

"I don't think you understand, I haven't had this type of conversation in five months, I want nothing more than to just keep talking," I said when I reached her. "Did you stumble into education?" I asked. I meant to see if she had other interests and was only teaching for lack of better options. Her answer rambled on and on about how her parents always stressed education, and when she never actually came to a point I realized here that she didn't have much in the way of working knowledge of what she was saying, only that her passion was guiding her to do well. That I suppose is well in and of itself enough.

She eventually found her friend and went her separate way. But I'll never forget the girl with the short black hair, sharp face, dark skin, and deeply fixated cat-like eyes, short enough to be a girl but fit enough to be a woman. It was refreshing to know that there are gorgeous women in the sea of madness, and some of them own meaning inside of their selves. It was nice to know there are people who care.

There Are People Who Care, Pt. II

There are people who care and there are people who don't care. It seems too often that people move from being one to the next. I think I have this effect on people. All the women I've known and loved seem to hate me when it's over.

It's not for anything that I say this. The world turns, souls cross, and the dust continues to gather when it's over. Along the way I'd like to have something to remember though. I've never believed myself to hold anything down on someone, and I don't have any hard feelings, really, toward anyone I've met. But in my life, when a woman leaves she is gone, long gone. So much so that someone I knew dearly for most of four years has demonized me in her mind. It's a rather bazaar concept, something I can't quite wrap my head around. To seriously think that I could take every bit of the happiness and joy that we shared, erase it and replace it with an image of someone that is so vile that I could never have spent such moments of excitement with them is an injustice. An injustice to both. My memories would be filled with sadness and regret and I wouldn't be much compelled to feel good about my life during those four years. Pretty incredible. I, personally, look back fondly.

But why does it continue to happen to me? Certainly I learned something from one woman to the next, even if only very little. It could mean only that there is something so deep in my character that it can't be fixed (to imply that it's wrong). I know that I am passionate; I know that I am idealistic; I know that I am demanding; I know that I expect a lot. These parts of me give us the best of times, but end in the most tragic of ways. The only way I see it – woman sees romance, falls for passion, wants change, doesn't get way, finds my unwavering drive overbearing, leaves. Usually they had so much of me by the time they've had enough they don't need to even say hello anymore, ever.

Don't get me wrong, I'm fine. But I can't go on in this world thinking that I've done these women, these human beings, wrong. All I did was love them in their own ways for their own time. Some for a day, some for a year, some for a week, and some always. It was what it was and that's great. What bothers me is that the same person who chose to be with me for a minute, for a day, for a week, a month, a year, a lifetime, could decide to quit and from that moment on tell everyone how awful I was. Surely that's not the case.

It could just be that I'm hopeful right now. *I'm likely not to see most everyone I've ever known ever again.* And I don't believe it's too much to ask that their memories of me be pleasant. Just because there's enough hate to go around doesn't mean we should share the wealth. If I never see these people again it should mean nothing to me what their last impression is – but then, that would mean I've done something, intentional or not, to cause them pain. And I don't want that. But yet they persist.

It could just be that there are people who care and there are people who don't.

I Wish My Mind

I wish my mind still worked like a child
Staring at a train not thinking all the while
That fire starts the engine starts the chains starts the wheels
But instead if I could drive how stupendous I would feel.

Watching mountains with their trees turn to grassy plains and
      fields
Sloping over hills coast to coast north to south west to east
Taking mail, picking boxes, making scheduled stops and times
Knowing only tomorrow brings another place to find.

But I'd probably hate it now thinking of all it would take.
From the amount of sleep to the amount of pay.
I'm not sure what's the bigger shame,
Never having driven or the chance I didn't take.

There Are Words

That fall into place and others that don't.
Mostly about the women I've wined,
The women I've dined,
And the women I've 69ed.
This is one of the damned ones that don't.
But sometimes neither do the women and in a way
It all makes sense.

Anything Simpler

If it were anything simpler
Than a smile and a move
I hope I'd have the answer
But street engagements are hard to find
And harder to work
When all you've got is all you're worth.

Sometimes I think the clothes I wear and the cigarette on my lip
Are enough to drag a stare
But that's where it ends.
I'm just a bum and I keep moving on.
Maybe someone will tag along.

Distraction

The blouse, the jeans, the shoes
It's a distraction from who she is
But walking down the strip we all want to be somebody else.
I wonder when we stopped just being ourselves.
If everyone stopped faking we'd all start making more love.

What Happened?

What happened to the whores and the music and the dancing?

What happened to the beer we'd drink, most of it dropped on the floor because I yanked her wrist and puller her out of the chair for a twist.

What happened to kicking her head back in smiles laughing at some stupid joke I said while drunk? It was the dumbest thing ever but who cared? It was obvious she was coming over.

Sometimes she would call if she didn't find someone else to fuck that night, but I didn't mind - it was still her voice on the line. Walking in, acting like it was me all along but all I wanted was her shirt off. What happened to fucking before we got to the room, her moans, our moves, backs arched when we both finish?

What happened to chasing love, feeling good, feeling bad, and doing it all over over over and over?

Where does she go when she's not by my side as the sun comes up so I can lean over and touch her breasts, up down up down up and slightly smiling with eyes closed because oops! I woke her up with my touch but she had to be going soon anyway.

What happens when nothing turns into something turns into nothing? It was so much easier when it was just whores and music and dancing, and smoke filled rooms with low hanging ceilings and endless possibilities and blues guitar and cheap beer and toes tappin' and chairs lining the wall and pool balls clackin' and no A/C and shouting to be heard.

Her Legs

Her legs speak my language
But they ramble
From her head to her tail.
It's all long sentences that catch me in the middle
Where the point gets lost
And instead of making sense I just keep reading until
She's out of words.
It doesn't rhyme but I love her verse.

Full / Half Full

The cup:
Full, half-full, empty.
Like a fuse that runs our whole life through
It's kind of symbolic.
A light that starts bright and ends without a fire.

We make so much happen when we're young
But one day we'll know that it's all the same
And it never ends in flames.

What The Fuck?

For PVT R. Landes

I loved her
    So I did it.
I loved her
    So we did it.
We were making love
    So we didn't think
That making love
    Would be the end
Of the life we had
    So I did it.
I joined the Army
    And she's far away
But close in my thoughts
    And dreams each day
And when it's over
    We'll make love again
As we once did
    Before I did it,
I went and joined the Army.
    What the fuck?

In Formation

The sun hangs low at the end of the day
And my thoughts are all I have as time passes away
To things I've done and places I've seen
While I'm stuck in one place and can't move my feet.
But the trees have branches and the branches have leaves
And it's their gift to put shade over me
As seconds turn to minutes turn to visions and dreams
Because I think I'll be here forever,
Or so it seems.

Push

From my head to my arms to my joints to my hands
It's one with the body and one with the land.
With eyes so close and near to the ground
I'm seeing things differently as if to be found.
But when my mind is tired and can wander no more
It waits by idly as I'm stuck to the floor.
Soon the pain grows until it won't even hurt,
I'll just stay here and wait for "As you were."

If I Could Say Hello

If I could say hello I'd reach out my hand and shake yours with exuberance, that same wry smile leaking out of one side of my face and eyes looking straight for the friends that I used to know, happy to see once again the people I shared so many memories with. You'd notice that I'm still wearing that same college ring as we shake hands, and maybe a few of the other things that are obvious – I don't have much hair on this head, which surely still brings me down every time I look into a mirror. My jaw and cheek line are slightly straighter, more slim, and bearing the look of someone who's getting older. My clothes are slimmer, too, tighter fitting to a body that's been working on improving, for the first time in a long time. I don't necessarily stand taller in these boots but I walk like it – because outside of the things going on you'd notice with your eye, there are changes inside that must be found with conversation.

Each time I see photos of home, certain cars driving by, hear particular songs, or think of special places, a person and a face cross my mind. Bittersweet is a word that I so often try not to use for its cliché, but it's possible that here for the first time it applies best in my life. When I start to get things I've always wanted, traveling, spontaneity, new environments, different people in different parts of the world, I start to realize what the cost is – the people that have shared my life with me. I've never been one to harbor any hard feelings for long, and I remember each and every one of you so well. From the smallest conversation with a schoolmate to the longest relationship with a lover, each memory is special and important. Without just one of those events in my life maybe none of this would've happened for me this way. So I want to thank you.

What breaks my heart is that that opportunity may never come for me. All the children I knew from grade school that have already grown up to marry, start families, have children of their own and make a life before me have so much going on that I could learn from, and surely my life could teach them something, maybe. All the wonderful students that I met at the university, watching young adults make mistakes and turn into teachers, engineers, salesman, musicians, biologists, lawyers, television reporters, and all around accomplish their dreams, are surely people that I want to hear from – their ability to focus on a single goal will forever escape me, and I want to know that they are doing well in their life. The friends that I've made through friends' friends' friends and only spent five minutes of my life with are equally important, and often had the most lasting impression on me. It's funny how in just one hour you'll never get to know someone deeply and how that fact opens up the chance for a simply great time, and how their smiles and jokes won't leave my mind. To the people that I've just said "hello" to on the street, or maybe met at the beach and shared a beer, I want you all to know that I'm doing fine for the first time in a long time and that it matters to me to hear the same for you. What makes me cry is that I will never have that chance with most, if any, of you.

What I'd start to say is that in three weeks I'll be moving to Germany. It's something that I still can't wrap my head around. I know that many of you have traveled overseas and seen amazing things, but I'll be able to not only leave the country for the first time in my life, but as a working adult, living and laboring in a completely different culture on the other side of the world. It's honestly something I've always wanted, and though I got there by no means I could've ever seen coming, the end result is still the same. I'll be able to learn and educate myself so much on the way that other human beings interact, behave, invoke religion, and love one another, in ways that I've never experienced – what wonderful things I'll see! So much of my life has been spent watching the show unfold before me, more as a viewer than a player, that maybe now as the journey starts I might someday find the place where I feel I belong. I can't be certain if that day will come but the adventure along the way is more important. So much of me knows that 24 years is young and I can't for one give into any account of the way this world should be lived – I'm doing mine, for me.

As I mentioned earlier, my body has been a focus of mine since joining the Army and I'm in the best shape of my life. Perfect? Hardly, but well and improving, that's what matters. More amazing than my physical self has been my ability to focus on my mind. It is unfortunate that this ability has been bore out of my frustration with those around me, but thankfully reading and writing have become a spiritual outlet for me, if you will. It occurred to me not long after arriving in Virginia that here and now in my life I am the only one responsible for gaining a further education. I don't mean in the literal sense, but more in the proverbial sense. Though I cannot attend university courses in person and gain the benefits of rigidity and graded structure (that would necessitate my need to study), I can still read the classics and watch myself grow with knowledge. I want to say that not much has changed, because I certainly don't feel any different, but there are times when I know I behave differently – when pressured or frustrated I am much less likely to react poorly, when depressed or lonely I am much less likely to seek a comfort mechanism but instead write or work out, when confronted I never yell, when scolded I never make excuses. This life has taught me that it too goes on, and each of these days will pass good and bad.

I can't mean for this way of life to last forever. Simply put, I've come too far and done too many things to settle into the Army forever. I might like the corporate benefits and the stability, but I can't stop this train and I won't accept quitting. When I get out I hope to have many options available to me, hopefully all over the world. Here I'm learning how to use my hands for the first time, rather than use my words; in fact, it's my words that get me in the most trouble here. But each day I get to wake up, run a few miles, and then get to the hangar to step onto one of man's most impossible inventions, a machine of flight, and see it carry out one of man's oldest and most evil of inventions – war. I may not agree with what goes on, but seeing the worst of man unfold before my eyes is a chance to grow that I need at this time.

And that's the most endearing point I want to make: *changing the course of your life is not a thing to be feared.* Its only costs are the friendships I had.

So if I don't get the chance to see you or call you often or send you emails or drink with you or even shake your hand, I want you to know that I really do feel awful that it won't come to pass. I wish I had enough time to sit down with each and every one of the thousands of people that I know and knew, and hear from you. Surely some of you are married, some of you have kids, some of you are divorced, some of you are successful, some of you are broke and homeless, some of you are happy and some of you are sad, some of you are in school and some of you are teaching class, some of you are living back home and some of you are in Korea, some of you are dead and some of you are living. *Knowing that those encounters will never occur is growing up.* But each of you has something to share. If you can't share it with me I ask that you share it with the world.

Howling Like Animals with Fangs to the Moon

1

Everywhere you look there's women,
Some old, some young,
Some beautiful, and a few ugly
But all of them will drive you mad.

The ones that always toss me over
Are usually seen walking somewhere alone
Taking strides with a purpose but no great hurry.
It gives the pretty ones just enough time
To glance over, shake an ass
And ignore me as they carry on
With whatever mindless activity they were most certainly
taking to another man.
Sometimes I knew it was good it wasn't me.
But most times I'd rather put up with it
If it meant getting a piece.
"Let's go to the beach."
"Alright."
"I'll do the cooking tonight."
"Okay."
"But don't drink too much."
"Sure."
And just as soon as she was content
I would grab at her breasts,
Lead her into bed
And bone one out
Maybe I'd blow my load on her stomach to be nice
Where she can clean it off.

But that's just a thought.
Most times they don't even wave
And I'm lucky I even got a glance my way.

2

I think she felt guilty, or maybe thought she'd fool me yet, but she called me back and this time just wants to talk. I'll go along with it, I thought, because anyone that good in bed once is just as good the second time.

So we met like two young lovers, a coffee shop by the river I'd never been to and she dressed like a woman I'd never met. Few days before when we met she was stone cold, tight blouse and jeans over heels that let her dark hair fall down her brown Mexican skin. Today she hadn't done her hair, had it pulled back and laced through an Indian print headband. There wasn't any makeup but it worked over the hand-stitched sweater, especially on a rainy day. It might've been two different women after all, but fuck it, or fuck her, whichever.

We started off around the river and I made the mistake of going sober. She got my whole life story. I can't be sure but it worked well enough to get her to a bar where I could drink and fondle her legs under the table. Just a little bit of romance.

"I feel like I'm giving away too much," I said.
"I don't mind."
"Let me take you somewhere."
"I'm along for the ride."

Never mind that we spent the night howling like animals, arched backs and fangs toward the moon. What I cherished was taking her to a saloon I knew, the last of the honky-tonks. A band was playing I had seen before and tonight was full of covers by Waylon and the favorites. I had to move a few chairs around in the back but it made just enough room for us to dance all night to the music, and reach over to suck from our beer bottles that we sat on the pool table.

3

I see faces and hear voices,
Elizabeth walking in front but turning her head back to smile,
Heather vacuuming the apartment in nothing but her yoga-
      sculpted body,
And oh that dark skin she was in,
And sometimes wish God had made memories more literal and
      with actual feeling.

It's probably better that he didn't, most men would save all
      their thoughts
For the touch of a wet cunt or a sloppy kiss
From a whore they can't get back.
Not me.
I always enjoyed holding their hands while shuffling our feet,
Sometimes in rhythm but always in style.
Anyone can fuck but not everyone can dance.

Usually if the mood was low, the blues lower,
The smoke would fill a room and all it took was "Mind a spin?"
      to get in.
Moving together was the best way to know someone,
Dancing was probably the best way to remember.

4

I don't think a girl ever left her panties at my place
At least any that I found.
Was I that bad or were they that good?
Somewhere in between I suppose.

In fact if I think about it I can see all their asses bent over next
to the bed picking up scraps of clothing. A few would stay
naked, grab all the pieces and change in the bathroom. A few I
can remember would always slip those panties and thongs on
first before doing anything else, maybe because they were
classy, or something like that. If they knew the way I looked at
them as they bent over, first dropping in the right leg then the
left, and doing that thing where they shake their hips from one
direction sharply and then slowly in the opposite as they slide
the cotton fabric up their legs, ending with a snap of the elastic
or maybe a tug with a thumb, they wouldn't feel that way. All
this detail would be so unnecessary if instead they never got out
of bed.

5

Is Manhattan as wonderful as it seems,
        Or as grand as they say?
I've never been there but I've always seen myself arriving on a
rainy day by a yellow cab across the Brooklyn Queens
Expressway. By then I'd have fallen into some fortune and
might wear a suit, dark, trench overcoat for the weather but at
the moment I exited the taxi no water would be falling and I'd
carry my things in hand as I walked along the buildings,
hopefully in no rush. Sooner or later, after a few cigarettes and
fake smiles, I'd come across a coffee shop, go in buy a mug and
sit down by the window along the sidewalk watching strangers
pass. The women with their high fashion, cell phones, and sense
of importance. The rain would slowly, slowly start to fall again
and I'd be forced to look out the window now speckled with
raindrops and if it came down any harder it'd be like looking
through a waterfall. I didn't have to be anywhere so I'd re-up
the coffee, strike a match and wait for the right girl to walk in.
Good thing I had some Mailer to read. The people just kept
walking in the rain.

I might like the city but it would take time.

6

Wake up, brush my teeth, get a beer, step outside, light a
cigarette, shower, walk out, find a bar, buy a drink, talk her up,
take her home, get a few drinks out, get her clothes off, get on
her, get off, go to sleep, watch her leave, wake up, take a
shower, get a beer, go outside, light a cigarette, throw on
clothes, drive off, stop at the park, walk around, say hello,
suggest a bar, buy us drinks, take her home, light a cigarette,
get a drink, grab her waist, lay her down, roll on, roll off, watch
her leave, wake up, get a beer, drink it in the shower, smoke a
cigarette, walk to the store, buy some bread and ham and
cigarettes and the daily, hit on the cashier, go home,
masturbate, answer the phone, "sure," grab a beer, wait, grab a
beer, light a cigarette, open the door, go straight for the kiss,
kick off my shoes, slip off my pants, grab at her panties, push
her to the bed, left her legs, play with her pussy, grab the
breasts and bite a nipple, lift her head and pull her hair, go fast
go slow go faster, "*oooooo*" she'd say, cum, go to sleep and
dream of her and wake up alone.

7

Men have always hated other men I believe.
Nietzsche said we'd come far enough
     That god was dead
     Or at least the need.
We're supposed to be civilized and democratized
And when you look around and hear the right buzzwords
It's easy to think it's true.
But women still exist, and a man still needs money
And wants success
So really we've just gone from
Fighting over God and land to throwing punches.
If you put your hand in the wrong place,
Maybe tried to spread some love where it doesn't belong
(spreading legs).
Or just aren't helping someone in the way they want
('cause we all want help)
And in a way that's no different than *jihads* and pilgrimage,
     just more petty.
So all we've added in a couple thousand years of humanity is
     awareness to our
     stupidity.
But then again it was only one man who said we were advanced,
aware,
And most people call him wrong.
I guess those people must be right if you really think about it.

8

It's been seven months since I've watched any television,
And while it's helped me to see clearer
The most noticeable effect is pushing me further from everyone
    else.

Seriously, I think the whole world is doped up on network
        programming,
The lines and characters pumping through their veins
Into the heart and up to the head.

It might explain:
1) The general lack of originality that comes out of their mouths
And
2) The reason they call it art, as if to justify their addiction with
a highbrow mark.

In truth there's no good art anymore, we keep using words like
"nostalgic" and "classic" and "pastiche" to recycle works of art
from the thousands, hundreds of years ago and suck out
whatever last new good inspiration might exist in the Mona
Lisa.

I hardly think Da Vinci would smile from the heavens on all the
plastic posters in apartments that somehow enrich this world.

I don't know what every painter or author intended
But I think they all at least wanted their legacy to inspire more
        art
Not recreations and facsimiles.

No wonder then that our modern television art is responsible
        for the death of it all.
It's just too easy to give up until you die.

9

You people love your cell phones so I'll make this comparison
      accordingly.

Women have antennas
Some you can see and some you can't
That receive the signals sent their way
And the older they are
The narrower the reception.

The younger ones had the slimmer bodies
More features too
But often never provided any focus.

They were all supposed to do one thing
And all still could.
It's just that some wouldn't let you.
You could spend time and money getting the phone to respond
to you
But not really.
If you just found the right one from the start, and took care of
      it,
It'll take care of you.

10

There's a pier over the water
Where we can't eat the fish
Catch and release
If you're lucky enough
To grab one out of the pond.
Fitting that it's sinewy green.
Deep, dark, heavy, thick
With the poisons they let sink all the way in
Where we can't eat the fish.

But I can go elsewhere
Elsewhere to eat
Because the earth has plenty.
It's a shame, this,
Or we wouldn't let the waters go bad in some place
And use other places to eat.
I drop my line in here to pass the time
And release the fish that end up just fine.
In a way it's like making friends
And surely then
I've found some good where things went bad,
Some light to poke through the dark water, if you will.
Maybe the fish are being playful,
Trying to hide but occasionally
Letting to be caught to remind me we all have to get along.
I wish I could play with my friends all day
But sooner or later over the trees comes the sound
THUMPA THUMPA THUMPA THUMPA
Breaking up the locusts and drowning the birds,
The helicopters flying their own sky
To tell me peace won't last all night.

11

So many body types but two-by-two we still fit together
Though one-by-one someone always pulls out,
drops out
falls out
quits to find another.

Like so many before and so many after but that's what makes it
        easy
To think about later when it's too late
"It was a mistake"
said by the time it's dead
And we're left one-by-one to wander around as a bunch of
        bodies
touching bodies
feeling bodies
piecing bodies together for just a minute to remember
That two-by-two is better and think that maybe two-by-two is
best for only a
        minute
Because one-by-one is the only way to go about it all
Even though two-by-two is the only thing on anyone's mind.

12

If second best has no rewards
It must be awful to be last
In a world with four billion people
Four billion souls trying to achieve notoriety
High or low
Just trying to make a name.
Last place or the darkest acts
Get better remembered for doing the worst
A way to see things that shouldn't be
But stuck in the middle gets no mention
Mostly for having settled and breaking no convention.
I'd like to think its better
One way or the other
To move one way or the other
To be hailed as a legend
Who braved to do well
Or braved to be the worst.
I'd hate to be in the middle,
It takes no courage to be average.

13

Where did all the feet go?
Marching down the street so often
With purpose
Trying to change the world.

When did all the soldiers quit?
Marching up the hills so often
Holding signs
Standing in picket lines.

The offices have not changed
Taxing us the same so often
Dropping bombs
Drafting kids for Vietnam.

Where did all the fight go?
Citizens never try so often
Like they would
When they were misunderstood.

Now the soldiers play the game
It's a paycheck all the same so often
Killing time
Without killing on the mind.

Hug the kids
Close the lid
Kiss the wife
Church on time
Cut the grass
Press the slacks
Buy a home
Pay the loan

With the paycheck they've been given
Holding rifles for a living
Asking
Where did all the meaning go?

This is not the freedom that so often had been said
Would separate the living from the dead.

14

Survival means different things
When you go from hunting food
To hunting Charlie in the woods.

We're back in Vietnam but this time
We're well fed
Because the taxpayers keep signing on
By simply signing off.

While the planes fill the sky
The human condition unchanged
Cell phones haven't given us soul mates
Bombs haven't given us cause
To stay alive any longer
If we've solved our hunger
To search for answers to the questions
No one ever asks
Because on the television they said the money would last.

15

Wheels in the sky rolling almost as fast
As the heads on the ground.
By now there's a wait at the pearly gates
So I'll then take my time
Before hopping in line
To determine a fate
By judgment that's not sound.

The people in line must be wondering
Where it went wrong,
If they quit too soon,
What their lovers will do,
And the longer it goes
They may never know
If they'll get a chance
To sing eternal songs.

So Dance! And play and climb the trees
Don't ever come down if you can see the forest from the leaves
And take time to die with the secrets you'll find
That we've all gone mad here on the ground
But nothing is as mad as rushing in line
And wasting your time
Waiting for a truth to come around.

16

As I was walking through the garden
That opened the coffee shop
Underneath a thatch gazebo
Sat a pink notecard that caught my eye
And for reasons I don't know why
I had to stop.

I think partly I wasn't ready to go in
And accepted the excuse to wait a minute longer
Nervous to meet for the first time the girl I knew two nights
      before
But also because my curiosity wanted to see
What the card was about.

Sure enough and without much surprise
It was a verse from the Bible
Written there in ink
"Only through Christ..." you know the one
And I wanted to reply
So I started to think.

Before I could write an answer the rain started to fall,
Inside I went without thinking it over
And she saw me from the corner
And I sat with nothing to say at all.

I was glad she was reading so I wouldn't have to say much
As I worked to find the right quote to be written down
So if again the card were found
The message would be said.

Of course she had to ask,
"It's something I need to say,"

Wrote down something by Heidegger like
"I became free once I gave up God"
And though I was afraid of what she thought
She put no expression upon her face.

In some weird way I thought it might impress her,
She was reading the *Baghavad Gita* for one,
But she also had a son
Which makes holding just that much easier.
So it's like starting over with her
'cause we were drunk that night
I think that's why she called me to spend time during the day
Hoping that being sober would give us time to say
Words that felt right.

"Is that really what you think?"
"I know more of what I don't believe in."
And the more I talked it became just a ramble
But something I hoped she'd see that these things were just me
And she wouldn't leave on her own.

And when she closed her book and began to shuffle
My nervous ticks started
"There she goes with her soft dark skin and deep, piercing eyes"
One of the wonderfully gorgeous one I'm glad to find
But always leave me broken hearted.

She got up, ran her hands through her hair
Turned around and smiled
"Let's go for a walk" as she pointed to the rain
And I got up to go her way
Leaving the notecard where it could be found in a while.

17

Bukowski was a dog
And Burroughs wrote about hell on Earth
And some say there's none worse than Sade
But it was Frost who said
"Nothing gold can stay."

For the man who led us down the road less traveled
That's a hard way to live
And I'd like to think
That such a short order on hope
Is no way to dream.

So give me the dogs
And the hell on earth
That I can find my way in their words
Because the pain of life gives pain to their lines
But anyone who says gold will not stay
Is surely doomed to the same.

18

Can we fall in love half way across the Earth?
Is that something that's worth our time?
Instead of trying to find love nearby
That I hold on
Through the miles and dream of her?

Do the circumstances meet?
Is that what she needs?

So many times I just want to quit
Trying to make it all work
Here or there
Now and then.

But then I'm reminded if this weren't so important
It wouldn't take up all that we think.

So love and make love
Failures come from trying
But so does success.

19

I wish I could write about ghosts
      And witches and skeleton things
It's a much better story to hear than
      "She broke my heart and left me again"
But I like to think I'm not alone
      And everyone can agree
That we don't all see ghosts as we know them
      But all are still alone.

My ghosts are the faces of the women
      Who haunt my dreams
I can still her their voices crying out
      When they're sleeping with me
So the tone they give is not spooky
      Or meant to scare
Because what hurts is the memory
      Of someone who shared
      Just a little bit.

From the attic and in the cellar
      And a few in the living room
All through the house
      It's all I can do
To take time each day to talk to them
      One by one
That maybe they'll leave (or come back)
      And my torment will be done.

20

Sometimes the sun rises on its own
And sometimes it rises
And it's for mine alone,
Gift-wrapped in a brown sack
I wish everything so lovely only cost a nickel.
But even words aren't free
Like all things that are cheap
It still costs something.
Mostly its time, and of course I mean mine,
I'll take out a loan for when the sun
Rises on its own
And save my time for when it's just my sunshine.

I don't need the car
        I won't own a home
Shiny things and diamond rings
        Never work out
But for 35 cents I can buy an orange
At the corner store
And in five minutes time I've gained
More than I ask
From a job that lasts right up to
        The day I die.

If I die every time I fall asleep
It's more important to remember the things that live and
        breathe
It wasn't me that said cubicles were suffocating
And if the odds aren't long
There are too many people
I could call me equal
To say I'm the only one.

21

America's coming of age has come and gone
Aged sixty-one since the day it was born
And forced to retire at 32
"We've done all we can with you"
And given a check to go its way
Hop on the bus and catch a plane
But no one was waving goodbye
When the wings hit the ground.
They stayed home
Not dancing to the sounds of a breaking news day:
"Two planes have turned day to night"
She was on board, alright,
Left us alone to find our way,
What a fucking way to die.
Good thing someone cried or I'd say we learned nothing.

22

...Texas on my mind. The dirty kind with the roughnecks and leatherbacks with back-strapped ax ready to till and hoe and make the spirit grow. The blade falls so smooth you'd never know that long ago we gave up labor for a filthy savior – that lying, cheating, soul-stealing taxman. I'm not a fan of the new way of living.

I'd rather buy a pasture and pay it with my sins. Life begins when it exits the dirt and hits the sky, and soon enough the fruit is ripe. Man, woman, and child are fed 'til death if their only debt is trying.

It used to be that all we'd need was a track of land, and by god our hands would make it work. No knock on the door for Chapter IV, only the sounds of the living singing like hounds for the tilling.

"Were you there when they crucified my Lord?"

23

It's too easy to remember the way
The steering wheel feels
But where is it leading?
Aren't we just dreaming every day
As we drive on the way to 9 to 5?
I spent twenty minutes trying to decide
To go in and try to make new friends
It's the living end of getting out and starting over
And reminds me why
We just keep driving until we can't get any older.
One after another in no direction in particular
And all I wanted to do was say hello.
I blame tomorrow for occupying today
And holding us ransom to the words we say.
No one listens but at least they hear enough
To know that when we go
We were pissed and living in fear.

24

I have to get drunk to write things down.
Does that make me an alcoholic or someone who's afraid?
Unimaginative or never made
Are the best ways to describe the words I pile on the pages
And the worst part
Is the celebrity I pay
Inside my brain
To keep the words fresh each day.
Even at a coffee shop
I never stop to think the girls won't watch
As my pen leads the way.
Good thing there's beer
Or else we'd all see we're nowhere near our dreams
And will one day be dead.
So barkeep! I'm here
Take my dollar and smile and pour and pay and change and
exchange and wave and let me sit down
To scribble out the words
I hope will someday be read.

25

Fresh water on the ground
But this time of year
Not enough comes down
To soak the cracks
And bring right back
The life that can't be found.
The soil's dry all the time
And all the crops die
Under sunshine
That any day other
Would feel like a lover
If it fell on shoulders like mine.
1 hundred and 5 never sounds right
But once in a while its fine.
46 days in a row crosses the line
And this time
The crops won't grow.

26

I don't like my handwriting.
Is that a crime for a writer to say?
I thought I'd be better
But the years will say nothing has changed
In the ways I script my letters.
Always been the same since the day
I chose to never know
The way cursive earned its pay.
But someday
I hope
The words will say more than their looks
And that'd be true if it were in a book.
I guess this is in a book.
I wrote it in a journal anyway.

27

Banality gets old
But coffee cups have soul
And old friends need something to do
If they have to listen to you.
So we met at the Monkey's Nest to wish each other the best,
Shake hands and spill all the latest plans.
Who's married, who's dead, who's living, who's rich, who's
     broke,
Somewhere ahead, somewhere behind,
     Just talking to pass the time.
And it surprised me how much we didn't know about the places
     Both of us go.
But it was better when the words slipped to value and worth,
     "What's the point of life?"
     "I'm okay with mine."
But is it really mine and what makes that fine?
Had to sit outside to smoke,
     Cars passing, people holding hands,
From the moon it must look like ants
     Crawling home from work
     To sleep, eat, and fuck
And wake up again
     To do it again
     And again
Without thinking then that we're not any better
     Than the change of weather that sends the birds
     Migrating across the world,
Probably worse.
Because we don't even leave and have things to see,
But somewhere in the middle of the bee line,
     If you look hard enough
Are two friends drinking coffee wondering how did we get here?

28

I know the answer is "getting older" but why must they go?
They smile as we shake hands but they always turn to walk
    toward their end
    And I'm left walking away to mine.
Sometimes I think it's my fault that I don't stop,
      Don't turn around and go the same direction,
      Back where everyone came from
And settle in right next to them, a safe place where things are
    warm and love is casual,
Filled with the hopes and dreams that fill the screen.
Just like the car they drove off in,
      Clean and new and pricey,
      The right one to attract the right one
And carry on home to make casual love that if done enough
Might end up being enough.
Why do I know the answers but keep asking the questions?
Why can't everyone come along with me? is the same as
      Why can't we all relax?
Why are there a few fighting when many are no longer trying?
It's the fire
An intangible desire to be fulfilled with more than hip clothes,
    Smooth moves, and a future with money.
Surely the land of milk and honey doesn't have strip clubs and
    golf courses
Where the two worlds are made that never meet,
And I'm left guessing what could have been
      If she had met him,
      Of if we danced,
      Of if we sang,
      Or if we cried,
      Or if we played jazz on the radio and for one day only all
the world tapped its feet.

29

All sadness can be shaken, taken from our hearts,
But usually with most success when we're taken from the heart
    of our joys, maybe our life.
Or at least the one we knew.
Starting new isn't starting over if we've learned from lovers and
    ghosts of memories past,
Left searing on our minds like the worst kind of pain but worse
    because the rain only stops when we've driven off to
    another place.
I can expect the same bars, I can live with the same food,
    But what keeps me up at night
Is sleeping alone because everywhere I go are the same people.
Beautiful enough to dance, lonely enough to make love, but
    scared enough to run home,
That damn place where dreams don't die but instead buy
    houses
And have kids
And work to pay bills
And for 75 ill years sit in the corner as a reminder that some
    people achieve the impossible
But I've chosen to settle with the typical.
    LIFE – 98 MILES AHEAD
The peddle on the floor and Blood On The Tracks on the radio
    and cigarettes in my hand,
Getting closer to getting farther away.
I hope when I get there the people like to dance, and just
    maybe,
That's a chance I'll take.

31

We met in a bar in the same way all good things come to an
      end,
With lots of drinking and loud noises,
Surrounded by friends and strangers,
Trying to dance to the good songs,
Shouting just to tell our stories,
Holding hands to get a drink,
Spinning to the fast songs,
Gripping to the slow ones,
Kissing to pass the time,
Saying nice things to get in line,
Taking pictures to remember nothing in particular,
Laughing at others just like us,
Exchanging numbers because it's the easy way,
Walking home alone because in the end it's the only way.

Sooner or later there won't be so much sadness left in the world
When people start doing something original.
It's hard to accomplish anything doing the same thing over and
      over.

32

I can't think of anything
To say
To feel
To do
To make this real.
These words have no direction
No meaning
No hope
No way of working well.
I'm leaving this town
For the first time
For a long time
For a good time
For a dream and won't come back.
But there's always a girl
To think of
To speak of
To dream of
To help pass the time.
They always come at the wrong time
And have me thinking wrong things
And mess up my words
And change my meanings
And I can't think of anything.

33

Right when it ends it starts again
But that's what happens when humans live alone,
They do what they're told.
It's a shame too because what we hear is JUMP
And do stupid things like fall in love because it's too easy to
      want it all.
I want someone to call
I want someone to rub up against like everyone else
But unlike everyone else
I won't pay with my soul.
And goddamnit if I grow old like this then and maybe then I'll
      know I'm wrong.

34

Breakfast is on its way
Too bad for me its supper
Having not eaten at all or slept at all
And unfortunately its not because I was making love all night
To a woman who knew my name
But instead because I'm on a plane getting farther away
From the only girl right now in the world who even smiles when
      I'm around.

And now she's not around and this could be my last country
      breakfast,
Toast and eggs,
To remind me of home.

So when it's gone maybe I'll have nothing to keep the memories
      fresh.
On the other side of the world maybe she'll have breakfast every
      now and then
And think of

Part II

LEARNING TO FLY

October 2011 – August 2014

These People Are Not Relics

These people are not relics. They can be touched, they talk and walk down streets just like you and I. Their language is different, and their streets may be cobblestoned – not bricks, not concrete, but real stones that are fat, jutty, and incongruous, the kinds that give fits to women in heels whose cigarettes fall evenly in the spaces between the rock, but I'll be damned if they don't keep walking in heels and they never stop smoking – but they are humans, flesh and mouths that work like ours but with a thousand years more practice. They are good at what they do and they are great at picking out the Americans in the crowd. These streets, these damn hard-to-walk streets have enough color and life to write pages about the feet that have crossed their lines, and they're filled with houses and buildings that look nothing like ours. Age is the easiest character to recognize, walls that are wooden and without symmetry, towering high at a minimum of four stories, packed next to each other like bundled sticks, smoke pouring out the fireplaces that see much use, doors that push in and coat racks in every room, where space is at a premium because the price of comfort is not worth the expense, but yes, absolutely, we will spend €2 on a *bier*. And when walking down these streets next to these buildings, the Americans are the loudest, the ones taking photos and gawking at the artifacts, each and every piece of a country that despite its duration seems funny or obscene because it doesn't use English on its signs or standard measurements on its coke bottles. The pictures are the same, but the language is different. That I assure you is the only difference.

These people pay taxes, too. Many more taxes than we do. These people use cellphones just like us, and enjoy a good ringtone all the same. They gather at coffee shops and talk about getting some, just like us. They go to the movies occasionally, drive BMWs, and they even like McDonald's just like us, even if it's not good for anyone. Even though it's in a different language. There are dogs that bark, stores that sell winter clothes, churches with bell towers, street lights that turn from green to red, trees that drop their leaves before the first snowfall, convenient stores with the newest Playboy, trains that run east to west, plugs in the wall, cash machines on each corner, and refrigerators in every apartment just like ours. They are the same human people just like us, but with a different language. After a few thousand years of doing it one way they've just learned to do it a different way, but in the same towns and with the same buildings and the same bars. Don't come over here and ask them how it feels to be a German because it is the same as it feels to be an American – a consequence of where we were born and in no way reflective of who we are.

Two residents of Nürnberg (Nuremberg) were kind enough to house me for a few days this past week. Oddly enough they were Portuguese, but very capable of conversing in English and even more capable of enjoying their time in Bavaria. Both are electrical engineers working in Germany for a company that deals largely with Japanese business, and have been in country for ten months and some days. They own their same Portuguese flair but eat the *schäuferle* and drink the *kellerbier*, and were more than happy to take us to the Zindorf *brauerei* to try each tap in the very town that they are made and sold from. We met Antonio first at a café just outside the castle and immediately he began to speak of the dirty taxes and politicians behind them, complaining that the euro makes less sense than the people implementing it. I expressed to him my shame using the English language, but he assured me that no one cared, it was the common ground for many people. Even the Russians that were hosted along with us. Or when their Lebanese neighbor joined us. In Germany. I think the only thing missing was a German. But as I am learning, they may not be the most outgoing.

There is a history in Germany that many don't want to remember, but most can't forget. It is the reason I wanted to see Nürnberg, "the city of the Nazis." There in Nürnberg were the very steps that Adolf Hitler stood on to proclaim the glory of the National Socialist Party, saluting over his troops in the Zeppelin Field in front of the pillar libraries with the swastika overhead on the roof of the building. And though the swastika was famously blown off that roof following the victory over Germany, the Germans themselves were responsible for tearing down much of the rest. The arena, once lined with stands and bleachers for 200,000 people, is now rotted and overrun by bushes and grasses and only a section remains where a soccer field has been installed, used by the Nürnberg American High School that was run by the American Department of Defense. A street runs through the middle of the field now and is lined with tractor trailers, where truck drivers everyday park their loads and get out to walk in front of the very place where World War II started and think nothing about it – it *was* once, but it is no more. It is almost forgotten, and would probably be gone if that, too, didn't cost money. Instead, it is for nature to ruin, slowly. The same is true for the Congress Halls, a giant horseshoe complex reminiscent of the Roman Coliseum, and the Luitpoldarena, where once was a square-kilometer of marching grounds and crested eagles but now rests an open recreational-park, with literally no remains of the concrete façade to be found, only the frisbees that have been forgotten by the owners of the dogs that now run its greens. Dogs that were taken out by their owners on a weekend, just like us.

And maybe that's one of the few things they've gotten right, and better than us. On Sundays no stores are open, but yet the people still take to the streets and patronize the bakeries and bars. They walk, they talk, and spend their Sunday simply talking about the night before and never think about staying inside. Why would you, on a day when there is nothing to do, do anything less than enjoy yourself outside? It's too easy to conjure, and where we are failing they got it right. It helps also to walk off the hangover. Here, the weekend is a day. Friday is spent resting because on Saturday, well, it might be Monday until the party is over. Drinks until 7am, food at all hours, girls smoking outside the doors underneath the signs and streetlamps, giggling with fever because maybe there is a man inside that will give them something, anything. It could be a karaoke bar, blues bar, club, café, dance floor, sports bar, or patio, and the scene is the same. People drinking and talking. Funny how humans tend to enjoy the same thing everywhere and all over the world.

This is why there are no dissimilarities. When I hop on the train to come back, there is a girl wearing a wool head-cover and white headphones connected to an iPod, square-rimmed glasses that catch her straightened brown hair, and pursed lips as she curiously leads her caramel eyes up and down my outfit, trying to figure out what these strange cowboy boots are doing on my feet. But her intent is the same as mine: go home, and live our life for another day.

Mata Hari

Dylan and I had finished singing our version of Elvis's "Hound Dog" and were heading outside to smoke, maybe just because that's what seems to come after everything. We left our Russian friends inside with the intent of coming back shortly, but through the red-lit hallway were walking two girls – and as the silhouettes turned into seductive, dark faces, the words could have been less direct: "You, are, uh, Merican?" Why, yes, yes, we are. And we'd like to make whores of you. The kinds of whores that don't ask too many questions except for the right ones. They met us directly in the hall after entering the bar, as if they knew what they were looking for and they found it in us. It takes a special kind of cunt to make it so obvious, and the taller one wasn't hiding that she was special. Our interest made obvious our intentions as well, but the only words were "yes." We were not so direct as she.

"You will take us to American then, make us wives?"

"Not exactly."

...

"See, you're in Germany. Why would I want to leave this country?"

"I have got to use the loo."

I wasn't waiting for that to end and went outside.

There we were smoking for a few minutes when, inevitably, they showed up outside – I'm not certain if they were drunk or determined or both, but after the usual round of "who are you" and "where are you from" she asked if we had ever fucked a German girl. The answer was no, but the words were "we'd like to." Funny how that kind of thing doesn't need to be spoken, but sure, go ahead and let them know. In the light I got a better look at exactly what was working me over. Sofina, the one with goals in mind, was taller than her friend, long hair that rolled with slight curls outside her eye line, painted green to match the outfit, and with just a bit of lipstick. I could tell all of this easily when she came up close, put her face near to mine and asked each question with eyes of a child, inquisitive but sincere, and slightly impressed that I knew a little of her language. She stood with her arms close by her side, but only when she wasn't trying to figure out to which side my cock hung. It was a nice game that I let her play all she wanted, hands down the outside of my pants. Would've been nicer on the inside, but I didn't mind a slow start.

What I did mind was the interruption. Inside were two Russians we were entertaining, and one I was hoping to make. Her name was Paulina, the exact type you'd expect – long blonde hair over piercing blue eyes, short and the right kind of body, a woman's body. I knew time was running short but they beat me to any type of move I could've made when they came outside and informed me that my other friend John couldn't be found, and they were ready to leave. Imagine finding yourself with two whores as your girl comes out, and, oh, my friend's gone. Thinking as quickly as I could I told them to go next door while I called my friend on the phone. Simple, get everyone moving before the girls get talking to each other. Dylan was left to escort the four of them to the bar next door and I just knew that Dylan's candor would work long enough for me to find John.

Lighting a cigarette I listened to the phone dial, and what I heard was the conversation in English next to me. John wasn't answering, his phone dead, but there was a new girl in front of me, the right kind of girl to appear. Dark, black hair, neatly trimmed to lay behind the ears, work blouse inside a peacoat, and a long skirt down to the slips, but beneath all this class was a cigarette in her hand – just right.

"I hear English. What gives?" I asked.

"Common language. We're from all over the place," she said. But her accent was native German.

"No, no, we just met," and she went on to explain the

male was from Ireland, the other female from New Zealand, and she from Würzberg up the street, her name Sophia. All of them had come on different forms of business but now were just sharing a smoke. I spent a minute yokeling the Mc, but it was the new girl I was after now. With just a nod she came over and asked me where I was going. Inside of course, to join my friends. She was doing the same, but had to be moving on soon. "Why don't you come with us," she offered, but I hadn't even been inside yet with my friend, and it was his birthday no less. Never mind that he was a fellow soldier and I was responsible for his livelihood after leaving him with two whores and two Russians, one of which I was trying to score. "Oh, I'll join you for a beer," she said. Make it happen, bartender.

What makes this bar great doesn't even start with the name, Mata Hari. Named after the WWII spy that played both sides until the end, it consists of about 65 square feet of floor space, and about 40 of that is taken by the bar. Throw in 25 patrons and you've got tight spaces. Naturally Dylan had taken everyone to the other side and when I entered I was stopped immediately with nowhere to go except sideways to talk to Sophia. It made things easier that way, but numbers are easy to decipher – there were two girls I could make on the other side of the bar and I was stuck here with this one. To make it worse, Sophia wasn't even trying to play hard. She had her beer held in both hands right beneath her chin as she looked directly up at me, like a child holding their most precious blanket asking the parents if they can sleep in their bed tonight. What's my name, where I'm from, what I do for work, all these passed over my tongue quickly, answering each question with a quick glance over my shoulder toward the whores, without any subtlety. Still she persisted.

"Look," I said, "I have to join my friend, it's his birthday and he keeps calling me."

"Can I come?" she asked.

"Why not?" I grabbed her hand and brought her over.

And there I was, one girl knocking down my door that I wasn't answering in order to pick up the other two. The one I had spent the whole night jawing, Paulina, was losing her patience with me – when it was just her and I we had it all - conversation, drinks, music, dancing, and her eyes into mine. It wasn't anything more than a game but the game was easy. I had to mess that up by throwing in two whores and a puppy dog. And still I wanted all their numbers. I couldn't think quickly enough. Initially I had to get back on Paulina's good side and show her I was listening. This of course was at Sophia's expense. At this moment I had to finally ask myself what I was doing. What worth am I placing on their feelings if I can so easily ignore and put away their conversations and attention, throwing about what they want for a minutes at a time just because I'm trying to distribute myself amongst them? Would this even work? I had to leave Sophia with Sascha, the male Russian, for a few minutes to get Paulina. It was here that I was given the type of distraction I needed.

I don't know if he didn't bring any deodorant or just doesn't wear any, but Sascha had an odor. It was bad. I don't know if he could smell it, but he could certainly see that in a bar where everyone has zero personal space, he could stretch out all arms and spin like a dandelion in the air without touching anyone. It was the biting, acidic smell of pure sweat, and everyone came to the same conclusion at the same time: outside.

Everyone started grabbing coats and drinks and soon enough were outside, but fragmented. Among them, the whore had found me first and began about her ways.

"How do I tell someone he smell?"

"You mean how do you ask, or you want to tell him?"

"Is there nice way?"

"Tell him he has an odor."

"Oh-door?"

"Close enough," I said.

Fitting at that moment she pulled out a can of aerosol from her purse and began spraying it about. Here I noticed that Sophia was having the same conversation with a separate group, and I had an in. After joking with her and explaining that I only knew Sascha through mutual friends, I wasn't to blame. She was laughing when her friends brought her coat to leave. Quick! "I need your number," I nearly shouted. She handed me a napkin that already had her number written down and stepped up to kiss me in the cheek.

"Call me when you're leaving this bar," she said. I knew I didn't have the intention of joining her that night. She wasn't the one that would give me what I needed, not immediately. She was a woman, not a whore. They were inside, and that's where I went.

The Horror

There was blood everywhere. The spot where our crotches met was red, solid with the blood that was leaking from her hole. Sophia was sitting on top of me, still leaning back with her legs forward and her arms in the air, trying to catch her breath after grinding my prick down to a nub. I had been leaning back myself, my thoughts wondering what kind of distraction I would need in the morning to allow me never to call her again after this, but, God, I never thought the answer would come so soon and be so goddamned red. This was not the kind of blood that I've seen when I started a woman's period early with a hard fuck. This was the kind of blood that comes spurting out of a vein when sliced wide open with a serrated blade. I was in the *Heart of Darkness*: "the horror." She was still leaning back and congratulating me on a job well done. I hadn't even gotten mine but the moment was no longer selfish.

"Sophia, I need you to sit up and look at me." She did so, not with much curiosity. "Look at me, Sophia. Don't panic. But you need to look down."

Her head went toward our genitals, my cock hard and still engaged but here it stopped. Her reactions were now more aware. "Oh, oh dear god," she said slowly, at once realizing something was terribly wrong, even if she couldn't feel it inside her. She jumped up to dismount me and there were our groins, each covered in a dark liquid mass making circles on our legs, almost like two lovers with identical scars. It didn't start too long ago I concluded, which was a good sign since we had been fucking for about two hours now. The sheets weren't soaked but they were absorbing the droplets of blood that fell from her cunt as she stood up and frantically began looking for a towel. She was apologizing as she tried to think, "This does not happen, this has ever not happened," in her broken English, unable to translate her thoughts to me in panic. Convinced that the injury wasn't mine, I was able to make one good point quickly: "Go wash yourself now." She stopped looking for her clothes and left the room to find the water closet. I was left sitting there on her bed, the red stains on my thighs glowing from the low lamp light, wondering how I had arrived at this moment. What could have possibly gone wrong, and what did I do to deserve this? These are things that happen, but this is not a good way to spend my first fuck in a few months.

We met that night in her hometown, Würzburg. Dylan and I had gotten off the train a few hours earlier and began with our typical journey through the streets of a foreign country – walking with cigarettes in our hands, hiding behind the smoke while we ogle the girls walking by in the streets. This country's people are every bit as beautiful as the hills on the horizon, the footsteps of the Alps just to the east. Today's main prize became a brunette that we followed off the train, sharp, glaring eyes like Audrey Hepburn, but resting on the face of a girl not a day over 19, about 5'6" and wearing jeans so tight you'd pop right through them if you had an erection. Her heels made her walk just right so that her legs, real skinny, moved with a shake underneath an ass so firm I could grab it with one handful. I shoved Dylan over and he tried to make something out of nothing, but she wasn't having it; seems she just wanted to go shopping alone.

After a meal to supplant the hangover from sharing a bottle of Jameson's the night before, we started walking in the direction of the river. Earlier in the week I had squared it with Sophia to meet today. We had met just seven days ago in Nürnberg, spending a few moments together that taught me just one trip to Würzburg would get what I wanted. She wasn't a whore, didn't have the build of one. She was wider, more natural; black, straight hair over eyes sunk behind thick black eyebrows. Attractive, but not a supermodel. It was the houndstooth coat and red leather gloves holding a cigarette that let me know she may have something, maybe intellectual, with substance. Her body wouldn't be hard for me to get, she made that evident. It was the intrigue of something more that stoked my curiosity. In any case, I was biding my time and in no rush – she had been at work during the day and what difference would it make if I got to her sooner. The end would probably be at the witching hour anyway, like it always is. When we reached the *Residenz* I decided to phone her. We were standing in an open parking lot in front of the city's palace, designed to replicate French capital buildings, and it just seemed an easy thing to do at the moment. She was at the supermarket, but would meet us later when her friend arrived from out of town. Dylan was delighted to hear this, so we continued walking through Würzburg on our own, building schemes about how things would work out if we were in fact to her friends back to an apartment somewhere. It was more than a desire, it was almost becoming necessity. The last train back home that night ran at ten 'til midnight, and we weren't the types of alcoholics to go home so early, with or without cunt. That meant if they didn't have us over, because no one likes animals running loose in their home, we would have to drink until the morning's first train at 5:00. We were only in Germany six weeks but this we knew already was not out of the question.

By the time she called me back we were lost within the city. We had no idea where the river was, or where we were. There were a number of parks, trails, chapels, and vineyards all over the city, each with their own particular intrigue. After passing through the central park we ran into a park area surrounded by wrought-iron fences where groups of older citizens were gathered playing bocce. Their metal balls were rolling along the ground and in front of us as we passed by following the sidewalk to a staircase. There at the bottom was a memorial, similar to the tomb of the fallen soldier – six stone figures in helmets carrying a coffin, a rather somber sight straight from a Dali painting, surrounded by giant concrete crosses all bearing a year from World War II. Turns out that toward the end of the German invasion over 200 British bombers leveled the entire city in just 15 minutes – the whole town has since been rebuilt to exact replications. So much for the "centuries old" feeling. Even the history here was faux, a gruesome one covering a tragedy. Despite this, we loved the area. Maybe it's being so new was what attracted us – the dirty parts of the Third Reich were buried beneath the streets, and here people could start over, had to start fresh.

Sophia called as we were reading about this history, but we couldn't give her any clue of where we were in the town – I wondered if I'd have been better at it drunk. She got tired of trying to figure it out over the phone and told us to find the castle, even then we bungled it and stopped at a church – I swear the buildings all look alike across the skyline. A gentleman was nice enough to tell me the name of the chapel and it was enough to get Sophia a mark on our location. I was buying a cappuccino when I saw her, wearing the same coat and looking around for me. Our glances met and thankfully we didn't have the "is that him?" glance where she might mistake me for not me. I was thankful I didn't do that to her either.

Her friend was more attractive. Darker skin, wavy black hair over a set of brown eyes, almost could be mistaken for a Latina, but her name was Christine and she, too, was from Würzburg. Dylan was excited at the sight of her. When Christine asked for a cigarette, explaining that she only smoked while drinking, and "tonight will be a party!" with hands high in the air, it was too perfect. If only I had known then.

"Should we grab some wine somewhere?" I asked, a bit impatient but mostly thirsty.

"We should wait here just another minute, my friend from out of town isn't quite here yet," Sophia responded. So it's not Christine then, the friend we were supposed to meet. Wonder what this could mean. Then, rather quickly, a girl walked up and introduced herself. A blonde, fully built with thick thighs, running all the way to her round cheekbones. Mother nature type. Klara was her name and she was quick to remind me we had met the week before. Could've fooled me, but whatever. She was going home to drop off a bag and so we left for wine. They led us to a German *weinstube* where I learned who they were, and I repeated myself to her; she remembered everything I had told her last week. I'm not sure that's a good thing, but it can't be bad. Turns out they were both law students at the university in town, and Christine was moonlighting as a tour guide for the castle on the hill, the big grand fortress that overlooked the entire city from the cliff. It could be seen from most parts of town, over 500-meters higher in elevation, but just off the river. When we walked by it felt like I was in a history book, seeing the students looking down at the text and images I too had seen so many times as a child – I was there, on that ancient river, in that ancient night, breathing and feeling and finally I was living. When Klara arrived we moved to the next bar, and I was living well.

There was something about Germany I learned in Nürnberg the week before, but in Würzburg it was worse. Bavarians, at least, love to have cheeky names for their drink joints – Bar Celona, Esco Bar, Rue Bar, RE Bar, Bar Code, and we must have hit them all. At each one these girls insisted we order liquor, and at every joint I made fun of Dylan for doing exactly that. Maybe because he spent his twenty-first birthday in Germany the week before, or maybe because he's that kind of flirt, but he went right in on it. All the fruits and colors of the fucking rainbow in their drink glasses. No, thank you. I'll stick to scotch and the occasional tequila. They found this peculiar of me, but every time they pointed out something "typically American" it was in Dylan's direction, despite my bullheadedness. Also typically American of him was his pernicious attraction to Christine. It was no good when she started mentioning her boyfriend, but it was even worse when Klara and Sophia were making sure she ate so that she "doesn't go crazy" with the liquor. That's a locked closet with standing guards if I ever saw one, but you can't teach a new dog old tricks, and he kept on. Fuck it, mine was easy and I didn't care what happened to him. Sophia got the worst of me and kept on coming back.

One thing you don't do with an asshole like me, especially while drinking, is ask him what he stands for. "You don't want to hear it," I warned, but Sophia asked again and Klara's puppy eyes insisted. Fine.

"I believe in people," I said. "There's only thing on this earth that makes us special and that's that we think we are. If we can't harness that ability, and touch the people, see the people, and learn from the people, we aren't doing a damn thing to enhance ourselves as humans."

"Is this why you go drinking with girls," they asked. So clever.

"I go drinking because it attracts my paranoia. There are things rolling through my head like a sledgehammer and when I'm out with a drink and good blues I don't worry about those things. For a few minutes I'm normal, and can maybe hold somebody. Outside of that, I'm not normal to anyone even though I'm as traditional as the Yankees winning the pennant. I don't watch television, I never get on the internet, and phones should only make calls. I prefer whiskey, dark beer, darker women, and good bits of wisdom that come to me while I'm smoking a cigarette. And if I can't do everything there is, learn from it, and provide something back to the world than I'm a failure. And drinking makes that pill easy to swallow."

They heard about how the world is a cracked safe with no money in it, how we've learned how to connect the globe and it only made us shallow, and they think I'm pessimistic if I can't just go along with the flow – "The world can't be changed," Klara said while looking straight into my eyes. Seems to me that's more pessimistic than trying to change it and believing I can. But I just drank my scotch. Maybe she's right after all. The good news was watching Sophia absorb all of this without running, and seeing that our distraction provided some good time with Christine for Dylan. But the talking was killing me, I needed a lay and heavy drink.

The next bar we went to was Tscharlie's, spelled in *Deustch*, where the old people went to hear shitty music and drink shitty beer. Perfect. The mix was eighties and funk and everyone's feet started moving. Over the next hour I learned that Sophia loved to dance, but to horrible music, and that she liked dancing in clubs. I liked her better when we were walking through the streets and she talked about the weight an entire country feels for having started and lost a world war, how the people of a city own the pain of being carpet-bombed for no reason, and how as a people they are resentful, out to prove something, even on an individual level. But I guess all I wanted was a lay, and I couldn't ask for the world if it comes so easily. So often the two never come as a package deal, and here was no different. She had her moments, but really she was like all the rest – studying in school to land a good job. How noble. When it was midnight the dancing stopped since it was now Sunday, apparently a day without dancing, a tradition still alive with the heavy Roman Catholic presence in Bavaria. I was disgusted at that notion, but took the peace for the night. Sophia replaced dancing with drinking and got more drunk, and soon she began to ask me sincere questions that I didn't want to answer: "Why are you going to Afghanistan?" she asked as she tugged at my arm. It seemed to me the kind of question a girlfriend would ask. Better play it straight.

"I want to see war. Here, where we are, freely enjoying beer, music, and the opposite sex is the best humans have achieved," I said to her. She nodded her head as if she understood. "But I need to see the worst also."

"You are so stupid," was her answer. She was probably right, but she didn't mean in the way that was correct. She placed her arm on my shoulder, and I led her outside for a cigarette. There we confronted Dylan and Christine who by now had become good friends, with him turning to me and giving me the look that said he was out. Fitting that he gave her the opportunity by looking away to come to us and say she was leaving. She took Klara with her and Dylan was left to his own devices. Nearing 4:00 in the morning we went inside to share one more drink at the table, my hand on Sophia's legs, moving up and down softly to make clear my intent. Oh, it seems her living room is available to us. How nice of her to offer, I said.

The walk back led along the river and there in the darkness was the calm I can never find. I hadn't been speaking much and their drunkenness had them walking forward without noticing I had stopped, but I didn't mind. It was more important for me to jump on the ledge and stand upright over the water's edge, the castle no longer lit for people to see but the silhouette barely visible on the hillside in the moonlight, the sounds of the water rushing through the dam and underneath the bridge, illuminating with the reflections from the lights on the houses that were mere meters from the flowing current. No one was out in the city save for us, and the world went right on by. What I was doing wasn't more important than the water's movement, so I saluted it with my silence. Eventually they noticed I was gone and had stopped. I caught up in time for Sophia to grab me by the arm and lead us to her flat. Up four flights of wooden stairs that creaked with each step we walked directly into a European flat, as I had seen them in the programs before: very small, and very crowded with the artifacts of their life. Sophia joined me on the balcony for a cigarette, and when we saw Dylan fall asleep inside we were alone. I knew I had completely misread her when I heard this: "I love the way your hands feel up my legs," in a low tone, sensual. Inside her was an animal.

"I've been wanting to do this for awhile," I said, and looked at her, moving in to kiss. It really is true that European women are all tongue. She went at it, without holding back. I grabbed her and she moved into my chair to straddle me. But it was cold out and after five minutes I suggested her room. We went inside, took Dylan to his bed for the night and went into her room. As if to be coy, she suggested I could sleep in the living room, on her couch, or cuddle with her. Whatever cuddle meant, that was I my answer. She began conversation as if we weren't going to fuck, but after two sentences she was on me again, but I learned it wasn't just an awkward start. The girl liked to talk briefly, a few sentences at a time, every so often throughout the ordeal. I didn't mind, long ago in the night I knew I didn't want to make her a girlfriend, or anything more than a fuck. This was confirmed when I saw her breasts, or how very little breasts there were. It was sad almost. Here was this attractive, intelligent female that, in spite of carrying a little extra weight, had none of it fall into her bosom. Of course it wasn't going to stop me at the moment, but I knew then that my attraction was dwindling. It was good, then, when I learned that she knew how to fuck. She was loud, and she liked to move her body around my cock, rather than have me do the work. It's always a joy when I find those girls. I don't mind getting a workout, but it's nice to meet halfway.

After two hours and a couple of orgasms on her part, that's when it happened, just as the sun was coming up. Her favorite position was on top, so that she could control the movements. She didn't go up and down as much, sliding her cunt on and off my cock, but more in the way a belly-dancer moves, rolling the hips to one side and then the other, up and down exactly like a cowgirl – so the saying goes. It was during one particularly sharp movement by her that my cock slipped out, but before anything could be done she moved back forward and it went back in, hard, with difficulty, like it was being pushed over the edge of a brick wall. We both carried on like professionals, because it was nothing new in the world of sex. Sex is a physical act that can require precision, but when you're howling mad and mostly drunk, precision is hard to come by. I just used my thumb to rub her clit and when it got wet our genitals began to glide more easily. And then the horror came, the sight, the panic, the finish, the rush, the cleanup. We washed in the shower to remove the blood, and everything seemed to be calming down until I had to tell her that she missed wiping the blood from her ass. She got back into the shower while I started wiping droplets from the tile floor. "You don't have to do that," she insisted, over and over.

I had to grab her by the shoulders and let her know that these things happen, that she needs to take care of herself, and that she needs my help right now to keep things calm. Until I had washed I was even worried that it could've been me that was bleeding, and when I pulled a big clot that was stuck to my prick I thought it was me – but there was no cut, no incision, no break. This was her burden, in her home. And after sharing something so traumatic I knew we couldn't share anything else or anything anymore. It was hard to even look her in the eyes, but I didn't hate her. We slept there on her bed, in new sheets, and for a while pretended like nothing happened. I woke up some hours later to the smell of breakfast. She had gotten up to cook a feast for Dylan and I. Of course he had no idea what had happened and I wasn't going to let him know, not until we were out of there.

So the last thing I shared with Sophia was a meal. Eggs, ham, rolls, and every kind of additive she had in the pantry. "Did I want butter?" or jam or honey or anything that could possibly please me. I ate my meal and drank my coffee, and did nothing to mislead her. Especially because every move I made was precariously watched over by Sophia, trying her best to please my every desire, full of shame for the events that passed during the night. She was noticeably scared, and I couldn't blame her. Just when she thought she had a little piece of romance it was taken from her. And I think she knew then that it wouldn't be the same for us. Good, I thought. I hope she knows.

It wasn't until right before we left when I went back into

her room that I thought she might've had a past with this type of thing. But there on the top of her bookcase were two photos framed together, each of the same thing, from the same moment – it was Sophia, a man her age, and three little girls all no older than maybe four years old. Ha! You got me this time, I said to myself. I said goodbye, and she kissed me one time before I turned to leave. I guess some people are better at hiding their intentions.

Always Doing Things I've Never Done

Always doing things I've never done, I feel alive like a skeleton ignited by fire inside the bones, burning through every fiber and using the heat to drive onward even when the body is lost. Repetition weighs like a chainmail over the ribcage, depressing the sternum inward where the lungs can't breathe, and after a long enough time the organs stop trying, stop moving at full speed and get accustomed to a long, lethargic process that keeps it merely alive but no longer living. Everyday and every week becomes a search for treasure, like Ahab at sea or Ponce de Leon on foot for the fountain of youth, trying to find the answers to life and the secrets of vengeance, if life is the arbiter and the only source of revenge is living forever.

For myself, the secrets are found simply in not standing still, not quitting to move and never looking back on the memories that play like ghosts on a television screen. Growing old is growing apart, and leaving behind the scenes of my youth for the script of my life ahead has been the most enlivening experience for me so far, one that will be requited only on my deathbed as I lay dying, clutching the infernal bastard that finally shot me down and screaming "I'll get you yet!" because if the afterlife exists it could only be used to move forward and away from the trappings of life on earth. But for all her traps and pratfalls nothing could convince me that a life not on earth is worth finding, whether in the physical world or the phenomenal. It is the soil that we spring from that must be touched, sifted between the fingers and heard as it drops quickly to the ground, the same way our bones will fall when the last shot rings out: the eyes may move skyward praying for an answer but the knees will buckle and the end will be met at the ground with a thud. Before the mud claims our spirit it is our duty to the air that we breathe and the animals we flock, the trees we plant and the oceans we cross to breathe deeply, dine sweetly, replenish and travel to the sources of these most exciting and unparalleled moments of transience, the points on the map that mark where human history took a dive forward, either up or down but always in a new direction and see for ourselves where we grew further apart from each of those tools that we use: the air, the flocks, the trees and the seas.

Once we were joined in symbiosis like a Mozart harmony, the tenors dancing delicately on the bedeviled and dragging basses that march the tune along. The animals could be counted on to migrate and with them the herds of humans would follow, and against the might of the struggle we would find trepidation and trials that wound us tightly to the core of existence: as one, and with all. Lately, though, the fields are marched by John Phillip Sousa himself – a driving rhythm moving at a slow, pounding court that never sways, never falters from the low-down, dirty depths of progress, sounding powerful and empiric but only at the expense of beauty and the beauty of non-syncopation – we used to find our way delicately through the mist, surely each person finding their own way. Now all we do is beat the same drum.

It all started following the war, that great event that tore everyone apart, or so they say. Really, it was a fight of global purification, the swift movement towards one world, one society that brought us together after tearing us apart. The Germans were killing for it, but the Americans won it. I've now seen what it means to liberate a country, and not because I'm at the front of the line holding a rifle. The past weekend was spent in Bastogne, Belgium, sight of the Nazi's greatest push westward into the American front and for which the Battle of the Bulge got its name. We were there to travel, to drink, and the relive the march that General Patton sent his troops on to relieve the small detachment that the Nazis sieged during the final months of World War II. Bastogne is a small town in eastern Belgium with a French heritage, settled into the valley of the northern Alps where seven different highways converge, a transportation hub that gave whoever held it access to western, northern, and Eastern Europe. It was here that the Nazis attempted to salvage their war, and it was here that I saw the Yankees coming. The people of Bastogne recreate the march and the singular battles that happened all throughout the siege on a weekly basis. And joining them for one weekend I knew what they lived for.

These people lived and breathed the opportunity to pretend, the chance to be someone else and the moment that they could be somebody important, as a symbol for their own freedom and the freedom of life. Streets filled with war trucks, machines, motorcycles and tanks from the American invasion and a third of every citizen in the street uniformed from head-to-toe in military gear, looking every bit as detailed as the textbooks that give our generations the perceptions we have of the devilish beauty of war that masks the brutality underneath. It was a sea of green and mud brown, rifles everywhere and motorcycles flying through the cobblestoned streets that overhead hang strings of lights declaring it was Christmas, that the soul should still be celebrated amidst chaos. At each intersection where soldiers (real and fake alike) gathered, there were conversations, drinks, and memorabilia traded, and slaps on the back with a hearty "Thank You!" to say that we're having a good time, but every smile and every wave became a moment hanging in time where I could freeze the reality around me and sink into the environment that wasn't truly mine, wasn't there for me, and became drunk when a salutation was returned with an honest to god peace sign from the hand of a man dressed as a Yank; it was my own moving picture, seen at the Paramount Theater in 1945. Knowledge learned is knowledge gained, and today's world is littered with the detached artifacts of things that were once but will never be again, attempting to fill the gaps with summations, guesses, extrapolations from what's left to figure out how the hell we got to where we were. But for just a minute I had Bill & Ted's phone booth and it took me to a place where peace was dropped and human lives once again could thrive.

The start of the march discovered for us the exact pictures that we were looking for but could never expect to see with our own eyes; the trailhead began at a Y-intersection and instantly I was greeted by a broken iron fence, only pieces left standing up at a canted angle where the chickens ran amok and squawked while running the other direction into the tall grass where the dew still sat as the sun slowly rose over the hills in the distance, every bit as if the war had just begun in this town and the walls were starting to fall from the firefights, the cold air breaking hard one direction and smacking the face with chills that drove the march into one of labor and not pleasure, the true source of liberation if no freedom was ever easy to find. And as the number of steps piled up the instances of war did also – intersections where barns were missing walls but inside was the Alliance troops ganged around, passing beer and smokes, smiling with their rifles thrown over their shoulders cheering that for only a minute they could break before putting their helmets on and getting back to business. And when it was all done, the uniforms didn't come off – the beer just became part of the uniform.

That evening brought with it the bars and the women, most of them in uniform, from soldiers to civilians they were dressed exactly as they were in 1945, farmers, panhandlers, shop-makers and shoe-cobblers all together under one roof to discuss the day's activities and the troubles of life that for once were no longer a problem but were at that time something to celebrate – should we be thankful for the opportunity to work a job and survive a family, we have something to live for if the opposite means stillness and death. There was the bleach-blond bombshell that looked like she came straight off the side of a B-52 Bomber, the type of woman that was found in the corner-store calendars of the time and the minds of every soldier, with names like Betty and Sue Ann, she stood five-foot-six and was every bit as candy-red lipstick and pouty lips as a fighting man could hope to come home to. Her friend contained the same eloquence but stuffed into tight-fitting plaid and farmer's overalls which were not enough to hold back the bosom that spilled through the sides of the shirt, a brunette this one but equal in passion with red lips and piercing blue eyes. Of course they spoke not a bit of English. Nor did their fighting counterpart – the kind of girl that you only see once in a few years, she was wearing a green parachutist suit and I'll be damned if it didn't ride perfectly down her backline to seam right at the seat of her ass and expose every inch and curve of what possibly were the only legs to ever make me cry. She too could only look quizzically as I tried to ask her how she was doing, but even just a hint of the French language from her mouth was enough to satiate my night's desire. Everything about the hillside and the women was perfect and perfectly disguised in a time that shipped us out of our being just like the soldiers they were pretending to be who were shipped overseas to fight for women they'd never see again, but maybe, just maybe, I'd see these women again because the fight for freedom is over but the fight for love never ends.

    This is enough to drive a man mad. It mostly drives them to war. I'm no different, but in between I take time to look at the river that runs through the middle of Laroche, Belgium, a waterway only a foot deep but riddled with a rock bed, no sand to be found so that the rushing water can be heard blocks away as it crashes around the corners of the centuries old wall that encases it inside the small town of maybe 400 people. The stone castle atop the hill, only a quarter way up the mountain but high above the shops and cafes that adorn the streets, looks down over the people as they walk to and from work, probably not for a minute to think that what they have is the most beautiful existence in the world, untainted by the hands of modern thought and civilized thinking because here living is not outbalanced by profit. It's a shame to think that they could be so used to the sight of the pines rising high over their windows that sparkle with the rising morning that they think nothing of it, because they do the same thing over and over again.

It's important to keep doing things differently. Even if the actions have similarities, it can't be a copy or facsimile of something that previously has never worked. But if just bringing a smile to my face is the end-means, there are many different ways to find this. Just keep marching, onward to new places, to new people, with new bars and new drinks and new roads and new streets and new languages and haircuts and numbers and dances and cuisine and cars and stores, books, colors, shows, and women, women with their looks that cut back from across their shoulder when you catch their eye as they turn back to look me in the eyes but they can't turn around to say hello because this world has business and it's theirs to take care of even though they could just stop for one minute and find that always doing things they've never done before might lead to something they've always wanted even in the face of knowing that the world says what we should do is the same as everyone, but doing it differently is the only way *or be damned.*

I Will Not Tell You That You Have To Go

I will not tell you that you have to go to Rome if you have never been. I will not tell you that you need to walk through the streets and eat the pizzas which can be found five to a corner while making your way to the Colysæum, or drink the wine that comes cheaper than a sixer of the local *birra*, or find time to check a map at every turn because there are many turns and each one brings uncertainty when the only thing certain is the opportunity for seeing something historic, important, trivial, desecrate, languid, luminous, pontificate, or even simple in a town where gregarious is the norm. There are no ways to be anything other than a traveller, an American, *la turista*, in a city where even half the Italians aren't from Rome and everyone wants to see the Vatican, Colysæum, Pantheon, Fontana di Trevi, the rolling hills of Trastevere that lead to the Santa Maria Basilica or the flowing walls that line the river and eventually lead to the Castel Saint Angelo or Testaccio or Piazza del Popolo where fireworks have flown, feet have tread, wine was poured, history was made, civilizations were born and thousands died at the hand of a belief or two. What's really died is curiosity.

Hopefully your curiosity will lead you to greater places where emotions still exist, where the world is singular and vast, where the people are harmonious and extravagant not for fashion but for living, where walking in no direction in particular and stopping for the first bottle of *vino* is more important than never stopping because dammit! we're going to make it to the Saint Peter's Basilica and see the fucking *Creation of Adam* inside the Sistine because I didn't travel all the way across the world to not see the world's greatest paintings, the world's greatest structures, the world's greatest history, the world's greatest women, the world's greatest church, the world's greatest tragedy. But the tragedy can only be seen if you take a second to stop and drink the wine, letting the people walk by, the time go by and the sun droop until finally around midnight the only people in the streets are drunk and they want occasionally, hopefully, to scream so loud that it can be heard up and over the open hole at the top of the Pantheon and down into the halls inside because at that time of night no sound is heard inside after visiting hours close at 6pm.

There is no way to experience Rome. Escape eludes at every turn because on every block and sidewalk and taxi cab and *ristorante* and fencing and park bench and lamppost is a man and possibly a woman carrying a map, a bag full of souvenirs for the family and the lost dreams that coincide with thinking that somehow "seeing" is "enriching" and nowhere in their bag or in their minds is the thought that this all means nothing and couldn't be worth the time it took to get here just to tell their coworkers how wonderful their trip was when they didn't even remark on the color of the bricks used in the streets (browned and black with age) or the shade of glass that holds the wine (mostly green with a few browns, too) or the smell inside the Sistine Chapel (like the first few minutes after a rainfall) or the way that nothing in this city will ever be as big as the impression we had of it before arriving. The Colysæum was in this way both full of awe and disappointing. In my drunken stupor of a four day bender that I spent in Rome I couldn't figure out what drove me to see the shrines, statues, plaques, lights, buildings, facts, things, nonsense until finally before leaving I realized that I did not feel like I was anywhere special or anywhere that I had not yet been. There is something to be said for the history here, that it is so great and so old that nothing I was seeing was I seeing for the first time. Sure, from the textbooks and the shows to the real thing it is certainly great, a checkmark to stage in my passport and a few photos to cherish, to make conversation at work and to prove to my friends in America that my time in Europe is not wasted. But I feel like I could have been more productive.

A few blocks walk and a slight downhill curve were all

that separated the Colysæum from my hostel, and surely did I walk the city as best I could during my brief time there. I've often learned that in my time around the world, before and after America, it can never be said that all was seen and all was done when visiting a city for just a few days during the week. So why try? Why burn your candle trying to walk to every artifact and edifice just to say that you've seen it, when all you're doing is wasting energy that could be spent drinking with strangers who might reveal something more genuine and honest than any thing that literally millions of people are doing at that exact moment? The Vatican had no less by my estimation than 100,000 people in it while I was there, and that's a tall order to handle for any moment of transience I might possibly have experienced.

There I am in the Pantheon trying to figure out why I walked into the Roman "Temple of the Gods" to see only a statue of the Virgin fucking Mary staring me in the face. There I am in the Vatican Museums walking at a pace that was determined by the flow of the crowd around me and not by my own desires, staring at Egyptian fucking hieroglyphics as if it were something I didn't pay money to see and *did* expect to visit while in Italy, waiting patiently for the Sistine Chapel to finally emerge along the tour, finding finally the Sistine Chapel at the end after the internal gift stores, reading the signs that politely asked me to "respect the Sistine Chapel, we'd like to remind you that it is a holy place," and staring guffawed at the ceiling that Michelangelo spent years creating while hundreds of people jammed into the room about the size of a barroom and listening to the yells, screams, whispers, and shouts of the tourists who were at a minimum every three minutes reminded to SILENCE PLEASE by the ushers who have no sense of humor or irony, one or both, doing nothing to stop the people from using their flash cameras because it's useless – useless because more important is the money, the tours, the profits, the glamour, the sights, because one church is the world's third most visited site not because it is holy but because it is historic (or ancient or some better word), but let's not blame the tourists. You did this to yourself, Pope. It could be stopped, but fuck it (€€€€).

There is no way to break through the masses, to grab the seagulls overhead and fly with them to the Mediterranean where I could drag with me the hostility, the vile, the darkness, the unstoppable capitalism march that has painted this Eternal City green and with it fall deeply, darkly to the bottom of the sea and plunge at such a speed and weight that the oceans would rise and another species from another planet might get to experience what is left from the tidal wreckage in the way we want to experience the streets of Rome – silently, from a distance, and with introspection. Somewhere on these streets walked Caesar, Maximus Aurelius, Bruno, Constantine, Da Vinci, Michelangelo, Raphael, soldiers of Rome, believers in Romulus and Remus, and making way to the present that we are given that in no way honors these great shapers of culture by doing anything other than making a euro off their name, and in a way that is not any way particularly surprising or tactful. Everything that was once inspiring and artful and paved at the hands of slaves and worked until the earth's largest buildings were completed was wiped away at the hands of the Roman Catholic Church, those devils who removed the great racing grounds where Ben Hur triumphed and replaced it with the Saint Peter's Basilica, the world's largest church which you can gain entry to for only 20€ (yes, I paid too, damnit). I'm not supposing that the Romans were any better than the Christians, one polytheists and the other monotheists, but at least they knew what integrity was. In this way everything became one and the same, and no longer contained any relics of exoticism, or that is to say, nothing that I don't feel I already knew about.

When I walk through the streets of Germany or the hills of Belgium or the mountains of Austria I see things that I am not at all familiar with, have never seen in person or in books, and learn to experience them in the only way any of us can – in our own moment, in our own history, and in our own mind. We cannot recreate the past and we cannot change the present, and in that way Rome makes its dollar – every corner with a street sign pointing to the nearest historic site that you have to see because you've heard about it so many times. More treasureful to me are the little alleys in Germany where houses butt up to watch makers and book stores and shops with *bier* and where people eat foods that I've never heard of and life is quiet because no one cares to visit the vast unknown, they only shop at Ralph Lauren.

By New Years night the millions converged on the Roman Forum, the ruins of the greatest halls ever conceived and used by the world's largest empire to make their congressional decisions. Millions, literally I mean fucking millions, of people together in the streets, not drinking, not dancing, not doing anything special – the music never played, the lights never grew, the wine was never poured and the people never laughed. Only when someone threw another firecracker underneath the feet of a girl did anyone get a jolt of anger or joy, only when the crowd was so massive that I made my way out not by walking but by being lifted from the sheer pressure of all the bodies around me, only when the last seconds of 2011 ticked away and only when everybody thought something might happen did they make something happen. There was no music, there was no dancing, just a few thousand more fireworks exploding at once, and not even the kind that fly but the kind that sit on the group until erupting in noise and without color. Some display, let me tell you.

It went on all throughout the night, all throughout the next day, and all throughout eternity did the halls of the homes and the streets continue to ring with the BANG of fireworks because someone didn't use all of theirs or they bought them off the nearest peddler selling light-up glasses, roses, fireworks, cheap purses, or knock-off watches. The peddlers were as numerous as the tourists, as numerous as the pizzerias, as numerous as the taxis, the hotels, the trashcans, the wine bars, the site maps, and the places where once great ideas prevailed but now only cameras flashed. I saw nothing resembling industry in Rome. Only food, hotels, places to sleep, eat, fuck, and spend money. It's what the tourists need after all and nowhere in the city center did anything else win, did anything else make money, did anybody have anything to say but "two for a euro" or "come and sit in our pizzeria," of course in broken English because there was no need to use Italian when even the Italians were tourists. This of course made it difficult to know anyone with any sincerity. No one cared to learn from, learn with, teach, or know anybody anything significant because no one had grown up and lived their life there. In fact, the most talking we did was at a bar in Campo dei Fieri, where the nightlife was most spectacular (but less than spectacular), at a joint called the Drunken Ship where hip-hop played and everyone spoke English. I couldn't avoid it because the people here spoke English, and those girls are the most loose, the most frivolous, mostly because they are just touring through like myself and because the women who weren't touring through knew that the men were.

Something about Italy I find striking is that their idea of a bar is turning a *ristorante* into a bar by night – nothing about the layout of the business is changed, just that the music gets louder. It is very difficult to talk to anyone that can hardly be walked through what with all the chairs and tables everywhere situated in a stupid line leading to a wall and the music playing so loudly that I cannot hear even my own voice. At least the American bar, for all its stupidity and the fucking sake that people traveled all over the world to see the Colysæum and play beer pong both at the same time, the music wasn't so loud that I couldn't speak. The one woman who gave me even five minutes was the bartender who had the day off, who had no one to talk to, and no friends besides the Americans she worked with. It was no different anywhere else. Stores, shops, eateries, all run by people who flock to Rome to find something ephemeral or holy and instead learn that making money is just as easy as it is around the world but twice as dirty. At least in the states we're not selling an idea along with our whores. That's the worst kind of bargain. It never fulfills.

What fulfills is life, grabbed vibrantly at the moment that it can be experienced (every moment, but only one at a time) and creating our own history. I like to fit in, I like to be simple, I like to drink and dine and dance and carouse and play and be and fight and breathe and drive and talk and impress and speak and do and sleep and walk and spend and read and smoke and touch and listen and feel and run wild in the streets just like a local, just like a neighbor who goes mad with the yearning for escape like us all but is trapped like us all, living the way people do where they live doing the things that they only know to do and do well and do for themselves but selfishness is the only way to happiness when nothing around us makes sense, so we drink at the smaller bars every night and the larger bars on the weekends and we walk through the streets stumbling on the curbs and laughing because it never gets old to forget the troubles, the torture, the ordinary way of thinking that comes with being human and being drunk gives us an edge to beat it for just one minute and think something grand, or sparkling, or set on fire. I couldn't do this in Rome. For as much as I tried, the closest I got was drinking wine all day at one *ristorante*, but even there the Romanian waitress, Alina was her name, spoke English in her jaunty way. It was cute at least when she tried to explain that a bigger bottle of wine was better only because it would get us more drunk, a motion she made not by saying the word drunk but by kicking back her head and rolling her eyes while smiling. I couldn't do anything else. Just drink and try to forget that I was in Rome.

In that way maybe I was just like everyone else in Rome. But I won't tell you that you too have to go.

I'm Going to War

I'm going to war. The dirty kind where souls are lost and life's cost is cheap. But everything will be all right. I am very real and so too is this world we live in.

As I write this I'm on a ferry to Helsinki, crossing the icy waters of the Gulf of Finland by boat to see a Nordic land, a Finnish people, something foreign. It was snowing this morning when I walked to the dock and I didn't mind that my head got soaked, coated tenderly with little bits of sleet that ran like water down my face. Soon enough the sky was blue and the sun came out. This whole springtime journey has been covered in snow, but I didn't mind that either – a white Easter morning in Salzburg, an unexpected snowfall in Prague, and long walks through Tallinn's old town with Jack Frost nipping at our toes. Frankly magical, unreal, sublime, and too much for my heart to hold. This is good.

For soon my heart will be empty and my head full of the burden of war, man's worst invention. If his best engineering has given us flight, we quickly strapped missiles on the wings and it's my job – literally – to make sure it is always ready to fire. And on the receiving end is no one, everyone, and myself. I'm aware that I could die, perish, and have left no great legacy near to what my dreams envision for myself. Somewhere in the ether I believe that my life will be remembered, like a sage, a poet, a muse, a thinker, and all things willing this will come to pass. Each living day after all gives me more, more breath, more scars, move love, more adoration for the earth in its entirety. But none of this would I have if not for war. So be it.

Nothing about my life can be wrong if I can taxi to Helsinki by boat, march the streets of Belgium, taste the wine in Italy, see the mountains of Austria, know the beautiful women of Europe, and be at once and for all abroad in the greatest canvas we know – humanity at large. But humanity demands a lot of us. To pay bills, pay taxes, raise a family, go to church, and consume us with enough nonsense to make us forget that life is a choice. I for one refuse to die slowly. This is the choice I have made.

What I'm trying to say is that I'm fine with the choice I've made – to go to war. Surely I will miss all of you, from the friends I've always had to the friends I've only recently gained, the family I've always had to the one I've not yet met, from the tender ones to the cruel ones, sweet to disparaging, courteous to inconsiderate, jovial to scrooge, rich to callous, ally to foe. I will miss you all. You have all played a part in getting me here, and for that I can't thank you enough.

What I also want you to know is that I'm scared this will be my last remarks. My greatest fear is that I won't return, not in this capacity. And I mean to say that I'd rather die in the desert than have my greatest asset ruined by war – my mind. The toll of battle has effects on everyone differently, but no one comes back the same. To think that I might lose my ambition to write, to speak, to continue searching and living for questions that have no answers, that to me is horrifying. What are we doing if not looking for the meaning to our life? I recently told a girl that I'm not a bad person, I'm just trying to find the meaning of being good. I know it doesn't exist but I won't accept giving up on trying.

What I know so far is that people are good. All across the planet we are not too different. Everyone is just looking for their version of love and happiness. Everyone is just trying to have something and someone to hold. If I've ever held you or been held by you, my eyes will never tell the full tale of the winds I soared while in your arms. We have only each other, and every minute is a lifetime. To ask more than what is present, to pass a day of love in want of a lifetime, is ludicrous. Get out there and make love one day at a time, it's all we have. Maybe eventually the pieces will align. But for now, no one has tomorrow.

And this is the war I see in people's hearts and minds. Afraid to risk the idea of a settled lifetime for the chance at a day's worth of joy or rich experience. Often these days leave with us a lifetime worth of impressions. But the battle against security is often wrought with shaking hands and indecision. Not to dance, not to drink, not to sing, not to bring life to the dull spectrum of living we call shopping malls and pool halls and court halls and downtown bars and church pews and HOV lanes and school rooms and conference centers and bus fares and garages and three bedroom/two bath dream homes and walking down the aisle – no, these things drag on like machines, and the ones who throw paint at the walls are carted off to rot in the asylum. But I say that the cure for insanity is not medication for a few, but to instead call all of us crazy. At least then we're on level footing. I am proudly no exception.

I'm now at a Finnish restaurant enjoying aged scotch, reindeer soup and veal top round, with a glass of wine. Where else could I receive such joy? Where else could I exhume the bones of the soul inside me? Where else but in the world could I be so alive? And how is it I feel like I'm the only one? No, I regret none of this. Not one minute. The battle I wage is not in the mind but in the desert, with guns and not with conscience. I've made peace with myself, that by making war I can calm my own soul.

Does that sound idiotic?

If it were not myself it would be someone else. The army is only numbers, only faces in uniforms, and I am only one of millions around the globe sworn to fight for whatever paper crosses the president's desk.

But I am learning.

My life individual is enriched because of the things I can now afford – world travel and unpredictability. This trip was put together on a whim, by a choice to go places and meet people and see again the most beautiful faces I know on this side of the pond. Everyone but myself went home to the states for whatever reason, but I spent 24 solid years there – and mostly I got nothing. Debt, heartbreak, cynicism, lust, debauchery. I can't think of too many things that were good during my time as a patriot. A few friends maybe. An education? I don't use it, at least not in the professional sense. And my friends, though I love them, are still where I left them. May the best come to them all. But if I never return I am sure to never see them again. This life process, the loss of friends and family through time and separation and not by death, is called growing up. If you're still mostly where you were as a child, you have failed. Am I saying I'm there? That I'm grown up? Hardly. Just that I'm trying, and being in another hemisphere is only a small step. *There is much to go.*

Even the desert is a place to go. Ten months in armed conflict should reveal a large nature of mankind and of myself. These things I want to know. I have seen Rome, I have seen Los Angeles, I have seen financial, industrial, and entertainment capitals of the world. I have seen the greatest achievements of mankind. But of the worst? I am a few days away. I am not sure if I will hold the hand of a dying soldier or see the splatter of blood on the ground. My job is not that close to the battle line. But, surely, it is still war. Even the chaplains aren't safe from the battle lines, and everyone changes, a little or a lot. How do I know? Simple – how many of you have done this? How many of you have risked it all to gain it all? Double or nothing. I'm rolling the dice.

So when you see me at the craps table of life, bet strong that I'll at least try. Maybe you can join me in the underground bars in Germany, or along the Salzach waters of Austria, or next to the Colysœm for a bottle of wine, or the beaches of Barcelona for sun and waves, or the Alps of the Swiss for the views, or the pubs in Belgium for the beer, or anywhere everywhere all the places that have and haven't been. Don't you want this? Am I the only one?

(I'm getting drunk)

I feel like everyone around me is on an assembly line, buying, shopping, fucking, breeding, working, dying, and I say No. JUMP OFF. Grab the nearest vine and swing like a monkey, for all your life depends on it! Act out, be wild, do all the things everyone warned you not to do, drink too much, fuck around, quit your job, shred your taxes and walk away, saying NO, I won't be another cog, I won't be another nail in the coffin of creativity. You have nothing to lose. Don't act like this is some minor preamble to an uncertain future and recognize where and when you sit as Life, capital L. Hollywood told you to not let it pass you by and I'm telling you sometimes Hollywood is right. Stop fighting within the system and start fighting the system itself. It starts by dropping everything you've ever known to learn as you go. Hopefully you'll go many places, each of them far away. That's where I'm going after all. Maybe it's easier when you don't have a home. I don't know if that helps. But whatever you do, skip like a rock across the water, landing new places but leaving ripples where you've been. That is something to hold onto. Not the people and the places, don't hold onto that. Hold onto the idea that moving and shaking does the whole world good. When you're smiling, don't say I didn't tell you so.

And if you never do, I ask that you not judge me. I've never lived according to the rules. So when its time to be rational, I'm going to war.

We Should All Do Something Fantastic

It won't be long until the credits roll
The curtain folds
And the story comes to an end.
Sometimes it seems as if this life is a film
Where the right lines are said
And the music fills the head
When two strange souls meet once and again
Halfway across the earth because the writer knew
That subtitles are best read when nothing makes sense.
And since I've never done anything crazy before
I JUMPED at the idea that
Hopping a plane
Would let me fly
Right out my mind
And into a place where snowfall keeps me warm
Because it, too, I have never seen and
Joy, too, I have long since had
But I just want a day, a single piece of time to say
"I didn't do it for any reason particular"
But just to say I did it,
Did something fantastic.
We should all do something fantastic.

The Sand

The sand....
The saaaaaannnnnnnnnddddddd on the horizon
In the noon of day it can burn your eyes
But with the proper shades it's quite a sight
To see it, to see it there
So straight, so wide
Looming like the tide but in fact infinite
In number like the passing of time.
Yet I, if I alone could walk far enough,
The sand would turn to grass would turn to water
Turn to wine to make it all divine.

So Much

So much, they know so damn much,
Seen so damn much and been so many damn places
And all I want to know is if they tasted the wine.
It wouldn't be so much to live a little
But I think it reaches a point where knowing so much
Turns a man into commodity.
A machine, if you will, not so much a pawn
Because they got here by choice.
Hell of a choice, I say.
One day maybe we will outgrow having to make that decision,
More likely not because we're living but because it's the end.

Growing Up and Paying Taxes

Everyone keeps saying to grow up and carry on
That living free and making love will get me nowhere.
"Can't keep on singing songs and doing nothing," they say.
But all the other options just lead to paying taxes.
And paying taxes seems pretty wrong to me.

Wanted to Say

I'm not really sure,
I never have been.
Certainly am not right now.
Certainly don't know why this terrible idea is on paper now
I know what I want to say
And I know what I want to do
But even when it's happening it's not real
Not in a way that I can make sense of.
There's the world proper and the world in my mind.
I don't often live in both.
Would you live there with me?
I think that's what I wanted to say.

Jesus, If You Knew

Jesus, if you knew where I was and what I was doing
You wouldn't thank me or anyone like me.
You might instead join me when it's done and
The end has come and gone.

Rusty Fingers

Rusty fingers on dusty keys,
Leading me, leading me
To type the words that come spilling out
Like the fog of an early morning slowly rolling over the tiny,
     little blades of grass that ~~glisten~~ ~~gleam~~ ~~glow~~ shimmer
     and shake beneath the weight of another day on this
     earth where things go terribly right
And things go terribly wrong.
It won't be soon before long that we'll know the clouds will roll
     away
But they won't stay gone forever.
The clouds have been and the clouds will be and in between we
     were.
Certain spirits see more misty mountains than others,
I believe they dreamed larger and lived harder,
I can't forget the feeling of these rusty keys, dusty keys.
Keys to living
Leading me, leading me.
Keys to giving the world a part of me so I might live longer
     whether terribly right or horribly wrong.
The only thing horrifying – the dust on these keys.

Something to Be Said

There was once something that needed to be said, but no one
said it. We all lost track of what it was and it faded away.

There were others after it, but nothing important. No one really
likes a loud mouth anyway.

But It Doesn't Get In The Way

Travel – (v; int*) 1. To go on or as if on a trip or tour : journey.*

Go your own way. Go far into the night. Go until the day lights and the streets fill and the signs read languages that you cannot read back. It doesn't get in the way.

Travel. Travel to places on the map you vaguely recall. Travel to corners of countries where information is hard to find, convenience doesn't exist, and getting around takes time. The time it takes will give you something to learn, something to see, and each challenge can be broken up by a good meal, a hard drink, and night of sleep. It doesn't get in the way.

I got lost once knowing where I was. Recently. Walking through St. Petersburg it took me two days to learn that "туалет" was pronounced the same as "toilet." For all the places I've been so far and all the things I've done I've gotten by with a strength of English and a dirge of Spanish, *Deutsche,* and the occasional "hellos" in many languages. But there, in Russia, nothing would save me. But it didn't get in the way. No amount of planning could've prepared me for how foreign it truly would be, in the streets, in the shops, in the restaurants, in the tramcars and taxis and museums and tobacco stops and cocktail bars. But it doesn't get in the way.

Throughout Europe it's common to speak English, the language having been taught in a majority of the schools for a generation or so now. It's not still uncommon to run into people who do not know English, but the running bet is safest that anyone my age can carry a conversation with ease. It's a bit damning, to be honest. To have crossed the Atlantic and learned nothing of the language of these people, to eat their food, know their women, drink their beer, watch their sports, and still... only English. But it doesn't get in the way. It's never stopped me from trying, and at times I've sat down to learn a little bit of *Deutsche* and Estonian and brush up on my Spanish. It helps when the hard looks of "you don't know any other language?" cross their faces. But even after six months living in Germany I get relaxed – of all the nations here in the European Union, Germany is by far the most educated in the English language. On their street signs, on their trains, in their bars, in the voices of the people – it's the language of their business. Probably for the American occupation up until twenty years ago do we have this to thank, but the idea is still: "you haven't learned *Deutsche* yet?" It never got in the way.

So I went to Russia. I went there and was taken back like catching a bullet. "How the fuck am I going to get anywhere?" I asked myself. Luckily I was making friends and got to know a few good people who were willing to help me out and make the time go by in the presence of something familiar. Because at first it was... frightening. I had to for the first time ask myself, "what the fuck am I going to do?" I wondered if I would find food easily, find drinks, be able to take a taxi, understand the metro system, do anything. Here in Germany, if one had a brief grasp of the basic words and street signs, it would be easy to at least guess the way around. But with words like "вход в музей," "10,00 с человека" and "Кожаное пальто" there is no guessing. There is no fucking way to get even close to the meaning of the words. I had to window shop for any inclination of what was inside. But it didn't get in my way.

Once I got used to the idea of knowing nothing, it was like starting over. What does the letter "____" sound like? How is this letter pronounced? Learning the alphabet at age 26. One by one and sound by sound until at least I could pronounce some words on the sign, regardless of whether I knew the meaning. As the letters came together, so too did some of the words. It became comical by the third day when I realized that certain English words were simply homonyms in Cyrillic, and that "ресторан [restaurants]" were actually everywhere. And once I knew where the food was I could go in. Sure, I was reduced to a madman's folly, pointing and uttering the few words of numbers that I knew. "один [ah-DEEN], два [dvah], три [tree], четыре [che-TYH-ree]" [one, two, three, four, respectively] and answering yes and no with "Да [da]" and "Нет [nyet]." It was humiliating and *I loved it*.

Because there's something about Russia. It's huge and it's freezing, but it doesn't get in the way. The sidewalks and streets are so large that very easily throughout the five days I spent in St. Petersburg a team of sweepers and trucks kept everything brushed and dry. And it was necessary because the snow never stopped. It is true that it was January 7 through January 11 but it is also true that it snowed everyday, and sometimes never stopped. I was expecting to see lots of snow, lots of ice, to feel chilled to the bone, but I didn't know what it would look like and feel like until I was there.

The moment came during my visit to the Hermitage Museum, the beautiful Winter Palace of the royal family that was erected in the 18th century and sits in the middle of town just across from the fortress along the Neva River. Inside the Hermitage I was enjoying refuge from the cold while touring the illustrious halls of royal artifacts, imperial dressings, and historical data amongst the unending flow of paintings of everything from Peter the Great to the death of Christ to a fishing market on a Saturday afternoon depicted by Peter Paul Rubens. The halls were winding, the things inside were blinding, but in the end it was the sight unseen that had me exit. Toward the north corner midway through the Hermitage I passed a window that looked outside. I saw nothing but white and was startled at first, not knowing what I was looking at. Was it a field of snow, had I become disoriented and was looking north into the plaza? I realized in short order that the river Neva, which I had not seen this far up yet, was indeed frozen thick over with blocks of ice for a stretch wider and longer than a quarter mile. From my side of Vasileyevsky Island the water was still flowing, nearer to the delta where the water broke into the sea. But here where the islands all met, the waters were still, callous and rocky like the surface of the moon, cold and white like the tundra. This was tundra. And to get out to it, to be near it, to see what such a thing looked like for the first time in my life meant to get out there into the cold once more and walk over the Trinity Bridge, the famous drawbridge in the middle town, to stand there with the wind whipping my hair and freezing my fingers, to slip in the ice on the bridge trying to lean over the ledge and see how thick the mighty water could get in temperatures below -10° centigrade – it got real thick. Jagged pieces of ice taller than myself were sticking up from the ice shelf, a collage of chunks that had over the previous weeks frozen up and broken free and smashed together again to form a floor that no man could walk. And as I studied the ice, mesmerized by its rough palette, its exotic formations, its foreign sights, the snow began to fall again. And fall and fall and pick up and fall and fall and get stuck in my hair and stick to my neck and blow nearly sideways as the blizzard picked up in kind. Planning to walk to the fortress next, a half-mile away, I was undeterred by the cold because it didn't get in the way.

With the proper coat and pair of gloves I wasn't stopped from sloshing in the growing floor of snow in sidewalks which only caused problems on staircases that hadn't yet been fully swept, making instead a slope better suited for sledding than walking. First passing the Rostral Columns, then the Stock Exchange, and then again over a bridge before crossing into the tip of the Peter & Paul Fortress to see for the first time where the city started. St. Petersburg had been founded to be the imperial city of Russia, the source of its beauty and wealth, the center of its attraction, the heart of Mother Russia. And so planning, it was decreed that the city would be seen from the tops of the fortress fanning out along all sides of the Neva, tall, glorious, fantastic. By the time I had made it to the fortress walls I had been outside in this blizzard, some -15° centigrade with increasing snowfall, for nearly two hours. But it didn't get in the way. I never even wore my hat, choosing instead to feel the wind blow through my hair and kick the ice off my head where it got stuck. And coming now to the walls along the river I paid my 35 rubles and walked onto the roof to see the famous panoramic. Breathtaking. Inspiring, really. The stretch of river here was a quarter-mile wide, but it didn't bend either for nearly a half-mile length of which the fortress was situated in the middle, looking both left and right where the city faded away into the snow over the bridges that dotted the river and connected the islands. The buildings that were five-stories high, each of them, all of them, all along the river forming a singular stretch that spanned for miles, made of grand palaces and picaresque storefronts, painted in various swaths of yellow and green and red according to their centuries-old tax code, but just barely a sight to be seen now through the winter, as if Manhattan were seen from across a Hudson River that had been stretched to three times its normal width.

Here for the first time I did not only see the expanse of this city, but I felt it. It began to sink in just how large the city, the country, the people could be and were. The largest country in the world would need an even larger city to be its beacon for the people, to be its center of attention. And at just under 300 years old, there now were some 7-million people living within its limits, scattered across the islands and throughout the channels, around the parks and into the forests that line the city's limits on the northern and western stretches, the pine woods that grow up in a place as cold and far north as St. Petersburg. But it didn't get in the way.

For 7-million people, I never fought for space. For 7-million people, I never got locked out of community. For 7-million people, I was never overcrowded, never confined, never locked in and crunched up, anywhere, doing anything. The metro handled the thousands of people that crossed its doors every ten minutes, the buses were large enough and numerous enough to handle the hundreds of people waiting on the sides of the street, the lanes of the roads wide enough to handle the hundreds of cars that now dotted the landscape, the surprising majority of those cars made up of American vehicles, large trucks and cargo carrying vehicles. The restaurants were everywhere and could handle the eating public, the sidewalks wide enough to hold the people that walked hand-in-hand up and down Nevsky Prospekt to do their shopping, casual dining, and carry on in the merry lives. Just as easily I could stroll through Alexander Park on the north of town and hop on the Metro at Gorkovskaya to arrive five kilometers south in the middle of Dostoevskaya just ten minutes later. The ease with which I could get around the city of 7-million people would blow your mind, to come from such a place where trains and cabs are the only choice and even they take half an hour to arrive. Here, the city was built to hold its occupants and serve them well.

But that's probably the closest it comes to serving them in some way. The largest relic of the Soviet era I experienced came in the attitude of the people. It's hard to explain, but it is, in a way, a sense of defeat. The ideas of change and combative choice seem not only irrelevant and impossible but unreal and nonexistent, a myth not to be explored. The friends I made were great, do not be confused. They were happy, and willing to help. There was a spirit of comfort and cohesion that existed within them in a way that I couldn't see in other places. They were readily available to help anyone out, anyone but their own selves. This I think is the reason for their helpfulness – they know that everyone is struggling.

If I asked them what their plans were and if they were happy, the response was overwhelmingly "what am I to do?" You couldn't change jobs or move around? "How am I going to do that?" Do you feel like you've been thrown into a system you can't beat? Again, "what am I to do?" The sense of oppression and control that existed (and may still exist) from the Soviet era pervaded their entire sense of being. It was as if they had been through the bottom pits of hell and emerged to be thankful for the opportunity even in the smallest way to live in some way with a bit of comfort, even if it was slightly predetermined. As if they were told at a young age what their direction would be, and having been shown an alternative much worse, they are happy to carry on in the line of their fathers before them and their grandfathers before that. "What are they to do?" I'm not sure. But in a lot of ways, it doesn't get in the way. Still, it has come far enough that they are afforded to live with their own pleasures in the forms of their lives. Bookstores are not censored, radios air freely, the newspapers present most of the news. They have the opportunity to at least live and eat as the first world does, with comfort, not in fear of death. Only maybe for fear of the government do they act timidly. But now with the opportunity to at least have some discretion over the things they do, it creates a compromise. Let the government do as it does, and leave me to do as I do. Only when the two worlds collide, "what are they to do?"

There is a strange bit of pride that exists within it. The people have come out on the other side of the communist era, still intact, still together as a Russian people, and now living well there is something to hold as victory within an identity. This pride manifested itself to me in the funniest and the most obvious of places. In each restaurant and at each Metro station and in any part of the city where I was struggling to communicate in Russian what my intentions and desires were, there was a Russian behind me that said, every time and without failure, "Welcome to Russia!" It was both heartwarming and unsettling at the same time, happily warm yet sarcastic, and it happened literally every time. I'm not sure how long that has been going on in Russia, but the presence of the phrase "Welcome to Russia" implies more, and anything but "welcome." Or, even if I am welcome, "welcome to a country like no other," or "welcome to the only place that matters." But, it doesn't get in the way. I never felt threatened, I never felt at danger, and I was never so severely mocked that I had to change plans or sit somewhere else. No, it was as simple as that – I was in Russia. I was somewhere I had never been.

I love going places I've never been. There's no more thrilling, satisfying, fulfilling experience in the world than to travel. To have put together a piece of life that has worked hard enough, fought hard enough, waited long enough to travel to some place of desire, some location of fancy, some town of whimsy, or even just to another part of the state. To obtain the freedom to travel by whatever means is truly serene when in the moments of our possessed transference to another reality, which is often the feeling when in such foreign locales. All the things that could go wrong, all the money spent, the time wasted, the flights planned, the taxis ridden, the hotels slept, the immense hours of go here and go there, all these things are nothing to the times I have when walking calmly, strolling pleasantly, finally and at once amongst a citizenry and populace that to me is new, different, exotic, enigmatic. The experience is dogmatic, in more ways than any god ever showed me. For all its problems, it's the only way I could've learned the things I know, grown the way I have, educated myself further without the confines of lecture.

And it's the north that does it for me. I've been there now in the spring and in the winter, and at both times it is equally beautiful. By north I mean far north into the Baltic States. I was going back to Estonia. I have a good reason to go back and a good reason to stay there. Every time I leave my heart stays back also. Such a wonderful country with such wonderful people, and every day I spend there is a gift on earth. Being so close to St. Petersburg there, I had no choice but to chance it in Russia, if only for a week. Being so close to St. Petersburg also explains a large part of the Estonian experience.

The funny thing about every country, at least here in

Europe, is that a great source of their pride is manufactured by reflecting it upon their neighbors. The Estonians are, for once and hopefully finally, free of Russia. Or free from Russia. For the greater part of the last 150 years until the fall of the Soviet Union, Estonia was in occupation by either Russian or German forces. It's really not fair either, being such a small country of just 1.4-million people. There are more people than that in the city limits of Dallas, Texas, and Dallas is hardly a noteworthy city. But take those people and spread them out over a country as large as North Carolina. There's a sense of victory, a sense of belonging on their own, a sense of being independent, and they strive to attain their stability through their own narrative. It does also make you wonder if they ever thank anyone for their freedom, given that 1.4-million people would hardly be able to overthrow the Russian government on their own. But it doesn't matter if they did, and it doesn't get in the way. Similar to the helpfulness of the Russian people who see that everyone needs help, the Estonians are proud to be helpful for the sake that they are free to be helpful, finally. In spite of their own opinions of their selves, they are nice people. Beautiful people also. Each and every one of them glows. It may be that irrepressible European spirit, the embodiment of living that gets Europeans outside and together, unlike the American spirit that separates and individualizes us. Because that's the only thing that gets in the way.

Somehow and in spite of our freedoms we've chosen to separate ourselves from the rest of the world, physically, emotionally, spiritually, ideologically, and live in a shell away from all the "bad things that happen out there." America is not candy land. But for some reason we think there is no better place and that each other country is filled with something subhuman, some facsimile of the modern man. It gets in the way.

There are beautiful people out there with bodies just like ours. There are intelligent people studying the same courses as us. There are hardworking people plowing farms and erecting buildings just like us. A lot of them still go to church (though not as many claim to be religious as Americans), and they still get drunk on the weekends and fuck. They drive cars, pay taxes, and do all the things that we all do and all hate together, and it doesn't get in the way.

Everyone drinks Coca-Cola.

But until you get out there, you won't know it. You won't know if you could find love until you go looking for it, even just by leaving your own backyard. America is a large country after all, a huge expanse of land. From one side to the next is a different mode of living, in the same way that moving from Latvia to France would be entirely different. But until you go, you'll never know. You'll only know what you're taught and that's things that are entirely wrong, entirely unproven, largely mythical and typical and horribly untrue. It gets in the way.

It gets in the way of traveling, makes you feel like it's unnecessary to move. It gets in the way, makes you care less for the water over the earth that feeds the soil that feeds the birds that fly in the sky that drops the rain that nourishes the grasses that feed the deer that feed the lions that sleep in the trees that shade the human beings that only until a few thousand years ago lived equally with the plants and animals within the system, this system of earth living.

You'll just never understand the world until you see it.

You'll just never understand the world until you see it.

You just have to see it.

You just have to see it.

There Was Nothing to Fear

"There is nothing to fear," he said to her
Lying there together in the night.
She knew the next day he'd be on a plane
But for the moment she felt he was right.
They had gone out, shared a few drinks,
Met her friends, danced.
They danced a lot. He thought they could've danced more,
But that's what leaving will do.
It will make you wish for more.

I Never Do What I Say

I never do what I say.
I come up with these wonderful ideas.
Things that sound wonderful –
Hiking the Slovenian mountains,
Writing in the bars of Prague, just like Kafka,
Walking the Villa Seurat and seeing the homes of Miller,
Hemingway,
Orwell,
Picasso.
Instead I get drunk.
I get drunk and I chase women, not always to success.
And when I do, I don't know what it means.
Does it mean anything?
I never did what I wanted.

Underground

Underground in a bar I had never been to
In a town I had never seen
In a country for the first time
That's where I saw her.

Years later she finally saw me,
But that was after we wasted the prime of our lives together.
There were cigarettes and mixed drinks and laughter in the
    early stages.
At one point we said, "I love you,"
But we stopped dancing and then stopped laughing and then
    stopped loving.

This Could Go Forever

This could go forever and
There's nothing here to be proud of,
There is nothing of life and liberty here
And still we continue.
Nothing of soul
No thing of spirit and
No where great minds yet still we continue.
There used to be glory where there was invention
And where there was hope and now there is...
There is only fame,
There is only laughter
There is only the end and hereafter.

Sometimes I Get Tired

Sometimes I get tired of walking around alone.
It's okay at first
In a new place to see new things.
Walk into restaurants, stop at shops,
Buy things.
Figure out what's next.
I always want to get a drink, find a girl
Give it a whirl.
But damn that gets old.
So fucking old.
I don't mind being alone.
I think.
I think while I'm alone.
Sometimes too much.
I always think I need someone, not really sure why.
No one's ever done anything for me.
Always me to them – time, money, love.
Give it all away and the only thing left is me,
Walking around alone.
Circles, it seems.
New places, same stories.
Am I different?
Yes.
But, I hope, not so much that I'll always keep walking alone.
From the top of a mountain it's nice. Peaceful even.
Sitting on top of the world, legs swinging free,
The people below carrying on their merry way.
Doing this, doing that. Eventually dying.
It's sad really that no one will join me.

I'm in a pizzeria in Ljubljana, Slovenia
With a hangover and a beer.
"*Laško*," it's not that bad.
I just want to share it with someone.
"It says lager, but it's a pilsner."
That's something I'd say.
But walking alone there's no one to listen.

This Global World

This global world!
Things we can do that we've never done,
Places we can go that we've never known.
By plane, by train, by land, by sea,
If someone can make a dollar they'll ship you for free
And it's hard to say who wins in the end
When money is freedom but work is no friend.

What the Hell Have I Done?

What the hell have I done?
I had so much promise.
Instead I'm the American Dream,
And that's no dream at all.
Anyone can fall asleep.

Go Down to the River and Pray

It is so hard to live with one's self in this world in these days in these places and in these rages from the fits and tantrums from the cages and ways they tell us it isn't good to be real. To feel something to do something to be something exciting and fundamental even or even just shoot out bright like a light on high in the night sky above where the dreams never reach anymore because everything is so deadly dead on the ground where the boys and girls make their beds these days, I can't see why I should join the procession of the unlucky fathoms of the deep deep deep down where the bones crawl and souls cry it's a crying shame that nothing ever has a point anymore and yet here we are feeling one thing and saying another and it's never enough to break the patterns or break our skulls at 90 miles an hour on the wall that we're heading into or did we already pass it? and now we're the walking undead or something that would fit into today's trivial notion of entertainment and stories and literature and literature and literature is it really literature if it teaches us to be drugged faces stuck to the television?

The words have no meaning here and no one knows really what it says except I and I and I alone are the one seeing or so I think and I wish I weren't alone. I wish I could bring with me all those daring all those fighting all those single spirits and ghosts and specters and even though haunting noises can't be touched and just float and never sleep and scream at night and have no end they are passioned so passionate so clear and have gotten away from a world that says "no no no don't do it don't don't don't this isn't right what feels so good" and we must forget that we have forgotten who the first one was to tell us that the things we want or the things we can't have and the things we do are the things that will damn us eternally in the sea of fire oh fire from the heavens oh fire from hell it would be so well it would be so.

So what is it? it's a trifle it's a duplicitous catacomb of wheeling drones dealing prone ideas that have no... future? heart? purpose? Do we have? Do we? What do we do when there's this over here that calls to our animal being true being you and I and let's go down to the river and pray.

And let's go down to the river and pray. Down to the river where I laid my body and saved my soul at the hands of the lord of the gods of the wind and the prairie and the sea and the water rising so high it seems like the great great great flood of bloody past that we say came one day to wash away the sinners from the saints and one day it will be so again but fire from the clouds from the dark dark storm that I hope is true because it would be so much better than watching us wither away like the leaves in the fall but they're so pretty the way they sprout, grow, green, give back and give back in the form of shade in the form of air in the form of one day another tree that grows up that grows up like we haven't imagined that it could be so wonderful that it just grows up on its own yes it does it grows so well with just a little bit of water just a little bit of chance and just a little bit of starry nights the stars there the the worlds and heavens spinning no not those heavens the heavens you can see they are real yes they are no not just one but many they are there you can see them just look just look just look just look please look up up up please look up the meaning of believing it ain't seeing and it damn sure ain't faith but that too you got to have if you put it in the right places and remember to pick it up on your way out the door.

With the keys and the wallet and in the mirror I check my tie to fit it right the Italian silk hand stitched black tie that though is different is not so different millions of years of history and humans and still we look the same and it's so hard to live with myself when all I want is a little peace of mind in a world at war.

War... wore... war. Like whores? maybe. Like... soldiers? no not at all we aren't fighting anything more than wages we aren't fighting anything more than pages from the book that Bernard Russell said "most humans are content accepting the series of circumstances around them as truth" and what a shame WHAT A GODDAMN SHAME because there is so much truth to be found we've barely scratched the surface and for the unlucky few the poor bastards who stumble upon just the tip of the top of the useless rot of truth it hurts much more to then be to then just be and to then be still in this world and still yet in another in another place that place where the souls want to go but get tugged back and forth back forth goes the tides go the waves surfing which we do more of on the web than in the water that covers the earth the beautiful salt that sticks your tongue and burns your eyes it would be so good to feel just a bit of it wouldn't it wouldn't it be nice to burn a little bit than to?

Go down to the river and pray.

There It Is

There it is
There
It
Is
Crashing with the sound of thunderclaps to say
Here I am
Here
I
Am
Some small, some large
But all grand.
The waves topped with white on the brown, sanded cliffs
Worn down from years of clapping
It's like shaking hands to announce to each other they've
    arrived.
The cliffs to be introduced
To the water not new
To the world
That should consider itself lucky.
Here we are, here we are.
Winding stairs for the man who sees
Not what goes on below
But what goes on in front when so much is underneath.
There it goes, there it goes
Back into the sea, back into the blue tides
The rising highs of water miles that keep us
Like a divider apart from our Mother Earth.
We should see her.
She speaks most when no one is listening.

Fake Glasses and a Bottle of Wine

Fake glasses and a bottle of wine does not make me refined
Nor does the notebook I'm writing in
In the back of a café
In the alleys of the former GDR.
There's graffiti on the walls but I can't be sure which is new
      but it all seems forced.
Looking for something in the heart
But how long until we find it?
Like a stolen lover
It's probably laying face down at the bottom
      of the Elbe
Never to be seen again.

Put Out Your Cigarette

Would you please put out your cigarette?
I used to smoke, too, pack a day.
      It just kills me to get that old scent again
Long sweet days doing nothing in the sun
Drinking all night and sleeping all day
Fingers slowly browning.
The time passes and eventually I quit
Now the time just goes by.

It's About Living and Dying

They say Hemingway was obsessed with death. To have given us Frederic Henry and Robert Jordan, two of his greatest heroes manifested of his own image, and to have provided them with only loss, suffering, and ultimately death, is an indictment on the statement of the creator's soul. Think also of Santiago for whom we met at the end of days, nearly ridden to the ground for his failures and who for as long as we know him quarrels at the lines of a marlin only to see his fate left in the bones on the sand. Or to have written a novel for his truest passion and to include in its title "Death." For this it could be construed easily for Hemingway as a life spent dying. But for those who find it, and I assure you Ernest Hemingway did, it is about *living*. It is about living and dying. A parallel birth of two extremes in constant dissolution yet infinitely romanced, at once warring and at peace – their cosmic values for it are then irresolutely entwined. The greatest of lives and the most rich with living often succumb to the most electric and brutal of ends. But for sake of the former we must suffer the latter.

I know this in my own way now. Not nearly as well as Mr. Hemingway, but in ways recently similar. The perceived keystone change in his life came at the events that inspired his first novel, *The Sun Also Rises*. I speak of the *Fiestas de San Fermines*. I know now because, like him, I set out on foot ahead of the bulls to see their passing and get a chance to place my hands on the fury of beasts. And where Hemingway ran with no modern records of safety during *los encierros*, I had the benefits of *los medicos y los policias* to guide the herd through a time-tested route where few among millions have ever been seriously injured, even fewer have died, and the chances of falling under those storming hooves seemed nearest to none. But I was wrong.

When it turned to look at me I knew it would be quick.

The next steps would occur in less than a half of a second and all that remains are a few mental snapshots obscured in my memory. The animal pausing long enough for me to approach from behind, my arm extending to touch it, the eyes that met mine as it whipped around, the head lowering, and the man to my side that got dragged to the ground in the horns because he jumped in front of me instead of the other way. I leaped over the head of the beast that was slamming its victim downward and didn't look backward until I reached safety and that's when I knew that to be alive was to be nearly dead. It wasn't until later that day that I learned I was dealing merely with an ox. I hadn't yet even seen a bull.

We woke up at 5:30am and in an hour started on foot. We arrived an hour early to run. We knew there were people everywhere but we didn't know the control measures. After trying two gates and still unable to even reach the fence line from the crowd we watched at a third fencing to see the gate open only for those people leaving. I spent the next minutes on my toes trying to see in. At that moment I saw the most beautiful girl in the festival – amongst a sea of millions, in a crowd of typical Spaniards with their dark skin and deep brown eyes, she smiled at me with her glowing blue eyes lost behind the soft blonde hair that fell like waves tossed in the wind over her shoulders. We joined everyone that turned toward the street when the fireworks went off. Screaming swelled. From behind the people on the fence all I could see were the faces of those on the balconies watching something pass through the street down below that I couldn't see or hear from the mass of the audience in my way. It was gone, I had missed it, and the girl walked away. Without any idea, lost in confusion and mostly regret, we walked toward the ring to find a crowd outside a series of closed doors, as expected. Only those with tickets were allowed passage, though we saw a few jump and run, and when we began to walk away, another swell of noise. Our reaction was *go go go* as the doors all opened.

Racing into the crowd and up the stairs was like all those scenes in the movies, the sun flooding so brightly down as we peered over the shoulders in front to reveal to us a gladiatorial landscape, the entire audience wearing white and ensconced in cheering on the tons of runners who taunted a horned animal below. It took me a few minutes to learn where to move because processing the scene required the extent of my will to focus. The frantic swell and swarm of hundreds of runners moving around and away from the ox with the fluidity of a school of fish chased undersea, the number of rows that separated me from the ring below (*seis*), the possibility of the police stopping people from jumping in and the fact that I saw none doing it, the spaces in the crowd that might give chance to climb below, the black man in the ring, long dreadlocks flowing behind a hulking body of his own, staring down three times the beast and holding still to grab its horns upon charging, throw his legs over and flip with the force of the oxen tossing him over its head to land, stagger to his feet with fists clinched in an outpouring of excited terror that he had survived, the rain of whistles and cheers that anointed him *el rey de los toros*, the red and green flags of Navarre county that alternated their way across the partitions of the ring, and the white, sweet white light that poured in like the sun must seem in the open air of outer space so deeply contrasting what can be seen and what cannot be seen that to focus on both sides of the light in the stadium simultaneously seemed impossible.

But there in the shade near to where I had raced into the front row was a boy jumping down into the ring at the objection of no one. *GO.* And I went down. Amongst the runners I couldn't see the animal, only the rush of people that would split to one side and then another. This happened a few times before I looked at *mis hombres Micah y Artur* and said with all eloquence, "fuck it, I'm going in." I was in a half sprint immediately because I didn't want to think about the alternatives of giving in, of having fear. The speed was meant for me to find the animal but quickly I learned that it would find me. As soon as the crowd would indicate to move in my direction the people in front of me would split and the charging beast would appear. I couldn't get in too close before the animal ran to the other side where it was corralled and the runners were left alone in the ring. Panic, confusion, did I miss it again? Would this prove to be my only opportunity to run or to even be amongst the taunting runners at the end who braved to slap the beast and I miss both? Catching my breath, merely seconds after the animal ran past me, thinking of the electricity in my veins, the reserves not yet spent and gaining a feeling of remorse when the pen was opened and above the shoulders of the massed runners I could see bodies enter the air, thrown up by whatever had just come out of the gate. More cheers flooded down as the runners scattered at this new, more wild thing that was parting the masses like the Red Sea. Whatever this thing was, it was angry. In merely a blink I saw it now, black, taller than the last and with hideous eyes that spoke of its own terror, and I saw him again, and then again, because he ran only at full speed and in all directions.

Watching the first and getting into the ring with another, I was learning and guessing that the animals would stop and in whatever direction they were facing would put their head down for a charge to that side. It made for a sort of figure eight around the ring as the size of the crowd of runners controlled the movements of the beast as much as the movements of the beast controlled the runners, a delicate tango between two compelling, different bodies of fear. And when the beasts would stop for that split second, that's the chance to touch it. This new thing with its larger, more upright horns never gave anyone that chance and when he did finally appear to pause he would as quickly spin around, dead in place but facing the other direction before anyone could move, bucking its head in all directions so fast that to be near it seemed idiotic or fatal. No one could get near it and it never rested. If I were lost in the back of the crowd in the ring I would lose sight of it and be caught in its way before I could react. To avert this I did the only thing I thought possible – get to a position where I could always see it. This meant to get close to the animal and run with it, a decision I made with more intent for survival than for daring. A chance! It finally stopped to catch its breath a few feet from my position, facing the other direction. I and the few others around me didn't hesitate to recognize this as our opportunity and lunged forward with arms outstretched to swat at its hind quarters. But rather than landing squarely like a palm on a cheek I could feel the grace of the hairs with only my fingertips because the beast had swung around to face me, to see its aggressors, to exchange blows. And when my forward momentum from reaching out had me just over its path and leaning into its glare, it glared back.

When the animals are about to strike their heads tilt downward and to the side. The force generated at the bulk of a scared animal that weighs over 1000 pounds is more frightening when its intent to harm is aimed at you. I got to this position in a matter of milliseconds, passing through the entire range of human excitement and terror as quickly as our heart can beat once. Reactions are impulse and mean nothing, the decisions our bodies made not concluded through reason or thought – there is no thought, just... electricity. When I jumped to the right at that moment it may have been because my left foot was already planted or it may have been because the beast had spun counterclockwise, forcing me away to my right. It could have been that by spinning around that direction the thing had pinned us to the wall and jumping right for me was a step forward now. Whatever the reason was that sent me that direction, it was the same for the man to my left who now passed in the bull's path toward me. That decision put him in between the horns, had him dragged to the ground, and left me with enough room to place a hand on the wall and leap over the combination of man and beast that tussled now on the ground at my feet. Never looking back while running, not making a noise save for the heaves of the lungs. Stopped to feel the sun come down and kiss my sweat-covered skin, dust-covered skin, to look up and squint through the rays and distinguish the bluest of skies above me, the ring all around, the frenzy, the noise of the lust of the crowd and the floor of the ring that had no air, all sucked out by the whimsical lot of fools that wanted to touch a pair of horns, maybe something greater. It all slowed down and I stood there feeling alive. I was electric and I was at peace. *And I was still in the ring with a horned animal.*

To say that it was an ox or something other than a bull, or to mention that only 15 people have died in the past 89 years since records were taken of the bull runs, or to hear that most all injuries occur from the feet of the crowd and not the bulls, these things make you think it won't be absolutely horrifying. There is no exaggeration meant when I say that I didn't know I was putting my life on the line. It all happens so quickly that there is no time to realize it could be the end of your life. But as easily as the terror enters your path it leaves again. In the end, the animals are as afraid as we are.

It's a mortal dance at the heart of it all. It's the cosmos swaying with the pull of a cord. That this chance at glancing certain fatality comes only with an animal partner is the assured crescendo in an already fortissimo fugue. Falling from the sky or swimming deep in the oceans or scaling the icy cliffs can all be equally ruinous, but their waters are navigated solely on the hands of the man at sea. He who imparts on these acts of bravery is testing his limits purposefully but stands as the only thing responsible for a doomed fate, should it arrive. But to run from the bulls is to have the marrow of your bones tested by an outward lethal force, the marriage of chance and skill, art and circumstance. You can run, but it can chase you. You can jump, but it can jump after you. You can try anything, but it may not be enough. So do not think that this tradition is carried out for its sole attraction or bemusement. *It is carried out because it merges life and death.* It is enacted year after year as a celebration of the brutal elements of living on earth, and for those that have seen it, for those that organize it, for those that participate, there is no other answer to the charge that it is cruel or unjust – it must continue. Everyone in play, from boys and girls to oxen and bulls, they all stand a chance at surviving the game of chess, the players all pawns moving in an *en passant* to escape the enemy but still claiming a victim, for the collision of such forces always has a victim. We have not lived on this planet so long to still deny the dynamisms of conflict that are as present as the sun always shining on some half of the earth at all times.

Isn't that just it? That sheer chance, a roll of the cosmic dice, produced for us a place so pure and bountiful that its harmony is seized only at the persistence of collision? Our fate is certain – we will all greet the grave. The equal forces of existence and nonexistence are constantly battling over control of the universe, and in the middle men and women struggle to avoid certain doom. A fool's struggle. If we exist only to come to an end, what is the point?

"Life has to be given a meaning for the obvious fact that it has no meaning," muses Henry Miller. "Something has to be created, as a healing and goading intervention, between life and death, because the conclusion that life points to is death and to that conclusive fact man instinctively and persistently shuts his eyes... Death then has to be defeated – or disguised, or transmogrified. But in the attempt to defeat death, man has inevitably obliged to defeat life, for the two are inextricably linked. Life moves onto death, and to deny one is to deny the other."

How sad then, how utterly tragic that the whole of the human race save for a few martyrs have lived then in sincere quietude to avoid a fate that is quite literally unavoidable? It is the most powerful scripts of the tragedians to quilt together the path of the doomed hero, the Greek titan that suffered at the hands of the gods for something as simple as seeing his home just one more time. We weep for the notion that our souls have something in common with Odysseus or Santiago, or even Raskolnikov, Thomas Sutpen and Jay Gatsby, or that possibly like the Oblonsky's we too have everything in confusion. To be like these heroes makes our insufferability and pious crawl toward death a bit more heroic. But such a thought, that this silly, stupid, inane, useless life we lead, the kind that involves the office and the cubicle and the computer and the 24-karat diamond engagement ring and 8-cylinder, 240 horsepower fuel-injected block and the three seasons, 24 episode marathons in front of the television and the late night tacos after the bar and the stored up vacation days to hit the beach only to go back to work again, that life, that utterly vain and callous life spent doing nothing, could even be close to something heroic is confusion of the highest order. And if we are confused it is only that we serve notoriety to those that live long and those that robustly serve up caution to be as saviors and saints, these men we call saints informed of the risks and still choose the safer path, one that is beset by the herds of men seeking to avoid the awful fate of death at the cost of an awfully robust life. But is it not more awful, not more wretched to see an entire life wane by untouched, unlit by fire, unmoved by any gravity to either side of the balances of life and death? To wilt away in the neutrality of fear? To deny life by denying death is to fall into the patterns of the wicked notions given before us.

It's taking at face value the morals of the unbrave who gave us birth into this despicable world. There are none yet for the recent generations who have come close to anything brave and we continue to berate those that try as outliers of a system that rewards only those who fall in with the tactics of cowardice. It is a true spirituality to embrace only the learned life, the kind that can only be reckoned from a charge towards the gates of life by charging at the gates of death; an acquittal from denying that we will crumble to dust elicits the truest understanding of God, renders the powers of the phantasmic and supernatural real and human, and there in our hands are the reins to Hell's chariot. The only rigid grasp of the infinite lies in the gripping of mortality, but even that can be confusing when so many misunderstand being mortal. Erich Gutkind offers a definition of mortality by way of explaining the Hebrew etymology of eternity, which is that of victory rather than duration: "to die means to be cut off, it does not mean to cease. One who is bound to others is free from the fear of death, for fear has its roots in separation. Where there is fear it is quickly followed by the flight to possessions."

But to hold onto things rather than seek the nectar of life, to be avoiding death by accumulation of mere things, that he concludes is a fate worse than any: "Far deadlier than any bodily decay is the death within our souls." Thus is the true spirit of the bourgeois, of which we all belong.

Throughout Pamplona existed the opportunity to reach forward at that new spirituality, to grab immortality by losing all possessions and running quite literally toward the horns of the beast, but all around me I saw orchards of reluctance springing up. Even for those brave enough to test their mettle during the running, they often did so at the patterns of culling those possessions that Gutkind says relieves our sense of being cut off. By saying "we've done the impossible" we can slip back into the comfortable confines of the resting bed of the weary to erode with the sands of time knowing that we lived once. I'm telling you once is not enough. Doing it once is not a lifetime spent in bravery. And in this day and age true bravery is revolution.

There in a city of a few hundred thousand existed for a day nearly millions. The sight was incredible in the dictionary's sense of being beyond belief. Within every footstep and every corner of the streets that maze through the city were thousands of revelers of the festivities, there in their white shirts and white pants, the red bandanas wrung around the necks and often the red sunglasses whose lenses were plucked from the frames to be worn only as a further assortment of red on a field of white white white white, everyone wearing white. It was beautiful, serene, majestic, almost holy. Every person had their individual manner of making the ensemble their own. I wore my blue flowered scarf rolled up and tied around my head, as usual, and often walked around without a shirt on. Even on the last day when I opted also for suspenders, hung down from my waist when I removed the white shirt following the run. For this reason I got a lot of color in my skin and learned just how curious Iberians could be about tattoos. For the women however their first and most utilized way for individualization was the size and cut of a pair of old jeans to reveal the ass cheeks. And I can say assuredly that there is no level of shame amongst them, many turning their jeans into shorts that rode up like damn near like a thong. It was titillating, but then again it also was no different than the rest.

There has to be a real search for the juice of the fruit to see the smoke from the fire. It would be easy to get lost in the rivers of sangria to miss the murky truths of the celestial battle underneath. The festival begins with the *Txupinazo*, a celebration of the festival itself without any bulls. Simply, the mayor *de la ciudad* pops off a firework to signal the beginning of the festivities which mostly means "let the drunk begin." This happens in the town hall, *Plaza Consistorial*, which is about 75 meters by 20 meters. But damn near every one of the revelers wants to be present, and that means about 15,000 people jammed into the space. The math on that breaks down to about 7 people per square meter, or, so tight you can't breathe fresh air because the bodies are packed so heavily that the heat and stench of shit piss and sangria wells up in a cloud above the crowd. Everyone gets by on the 1-liter bottles of sangria, all the same bottles, and drinks to excess *antes de mediodia*. The girls begin to jump on the shoulders of the men and it quickly devolves into low-grade sexual assault, the game of "you can't get up on the shoulders if you're not taking your shirt off" becomes "we're ripping your shirt off." And it doesn't stop them, they keep jumping up there and laughing while clutching their chest to tease the masses that maybe their breasts won't come out, an inevitable falsity. The least that can be done in any situation is to throw sangria in all directions until the shirts fade to a soaked shade of pink, the skin dripping with the sticky sweet wine more than any sweat from the collusion of bodies.

This goes on for hours before the mayor comes out, the focus of the crowd switching from one atrocity to another. It's more colorful still in the depths of drunkenness when, say, a woman steps out on an overlooking balcony from an apartment in the buildings but does not unveil her bosom, and soon the sangria bottles take flight. It looks like an open bag of popcorn popping over a fire, nearly hundreds of plastic bottles flying up and down in one direction until the crowd gets what it wants. Cheers of songs, singing, goddamned singing of that groove line "Seven Nation Army" that has so swept the European nations, and devolution of the worst kind as if lurking amongst the rats of a sewer. The crowd is so tight that any movement creates a push so intense that it seems like being pushed into a wall by a thousand people. The feet are so tight together that people lean over and on top of each other because there is nowhere to step. Worse yet, my shoelaces had come undone in the scrum and every time someone else stepped on them I was at the mercy of the crowd to stay above ground level. There were others who couldn't. Eventually the mayor came out to the chanting of *Viva la San Fermin! Viva la San Fermin!* as everyone raises their red bandanas to put them on for the first time. And in a flash of a single firework the crowd begins to spread out to celebrate amongst the streets, to find the bars, to quench the anger of a feisty drunk in the cafes prepared to meet a mob, and the pressure of the outgoing crowd pushed me in a direction other than my choosing. It turned out to be fortuitous as those watching on the balconies took to tossing water on the already soaked masses below who welcomed the bath like a freedom from oppression. I was pushed into the next block where a group of onlookers on the balcony had arranged a running hose and a few buckets of water, and there we took to dancing in the shower that rained down below. And like all previous situations, the attractive woman amongst the crowd above who wouldn't emerge was taunted with chants of "*Punta! Eh perra! Viene extiorora!*" until she danced her way into the vision of the crowds, eliciting their cheers. She too began to dump water on us with a smile and the ritual was complete.

In these rich waters of the murky greens floats the relics of *la verdad*. There are not many chances in a lifetime to be so submerged in the presence of the people. To be so utterly thrust into their whimsy, their phantasmagoric, principled mastication of the realms of the dire, wearied exhaustion and consumption of the soul. The way without provocation that a mass of so many can simultaneously engage in the act of release, to the see the physical and spiritual exile from the chains of reality if only for a day. To know that all day and everywhere there are people celebrating for celebrating's sake, that the cause of the gathering centers around the act of one man taunting death with horns. Others are living from relishing that others might die. And for many the opportunity to do the same comes from the ability to be put in the way of the bulls during the runs. Or even, to create an environment where any such examination of bravado is not out of question.

Our first night in the city was spent familiarizing our way around so that we might better be prepared for the frenzy ahead and in the wanderings through the street we encountered an enthusiastic bloke from Ireland here for his second run in as many years. The lad was our age, blonde dreads pulled up in a bun and without a shirt, speaking through a thick accent and a drunk that were both appropriately Irish. He made it quickly apparent that his experience in the runs before made him somewhat of a savant, an idea that I was not quick to absorb but neither hasty to dismiss. To learn something from a soul who had at least run once might reveal to me something necessary that cannot be learned from observation or research. "Rule number one," he shouted out the side of his mouth, "if ya go dow'un, stay the fuck dow'un." I thought he meant from the bulls but his repetition of the phrase implied that for any reason not to get up. "Rule number two, if it's your first run, dow'unt run the curve," he said more somberly. "Dow'unt run the fucking curve. You're not a fucking hero, dow'unt run the curve."

As we plodded through the inquisitions and information we reached a more subtle moment in his haranguing of the festival, one of proud dissonance if someone can be so delighted to know something that seems wrong. There is apparently something called the fountain jump amongst those who've heard of its existence. It is exactly as it sounds, people jumping from a fountain. Although it's more of a monument than a statue or fountain. "Something that all the locals hate is the fountain jump," he shouted while pointing down the block. "The Aussie's came up with this fucking great idea of falling off this fountain into the arms of their drunk brothers, I mean a literal fucking fall off of a fountain into four guys holding their hands together," he said. The pantomime included slamming his hand into the ground with a loud slap. "Literally more people get hurt on the fountain jump every year than the bull runs. I mean you're falling arms wide on the pavement at full speed, it's fucking stupid." And so I knew where to find myself after the *Txupinazo* dissolved, and so coincidentally was pushed directly there in the proceeding minutes. And what a fucking idiot to get on top of this concrete ball and do a trust fall from 20 feet up. In the condition everyone was in it was a nigh miracle that no one died on that day. I saw a man get lifted up, give himself a half-hearted *esprit tu santé* before tossing his cigarette, placing his hands across his chest and falling into the arms below. God they caught him but he hit them with a force like a car crash. It may have been the most daring thing I saw all weekend and one fountain jump was enough. The rest was spent in a merry wandering about the town with the muse of San Fermin. God, what a muse.

The streets were made of large, slick brick stones that made for a marble-top similar to skating on ice for the first time. The tide of booze and excrement from the horde covered the street entire and left no space in the city the sanctity of going untouched. It reeked of the stench of a waste treatment facility on a hot day and yet the people seemed not in the least bit phased. The merriment continued at full speed, a raging, pulsating gush of vivacity that spread from the town hall in all directions like a wild plague picking up more victims as it sprawled outward. There was so much white and red, not a single person daring to wear anything other. And for everyone there was rejoicing. It was impossible to not be elated at the massive undertaking.

It was a massive undertaking all at once, after all. That so many could so impulsively join in a swarthy jamboree was a marvel worthy of highest praise of historical reflection. But that too for itself is astonishing and depressing – the behavior is so coordinated, so predictive, so ostensive that it can make for anyone present enough distraction to disguise the beauty below. *We were there to put life on the precipice of judgment.* But for too many it was just another check in the list of bourgeois accomplishments that reflect on a life well lived. If only they knew that a quiet death indicated a quiet life!

Everywhere short white shorts that carried the beautiful, tanned legs of the whores that wandered around, eyes peering out at the gathered multitudes who served back the obvious mark, the competition of each other to outdo and be outdone by the best, to drink and dance and drink and drink and drink drink drink and throw the glass on the ground it was too far away to the trash can and too easy to buy a drink from the outdoor bar or the waiter walking by or the storefront next door or from the beggars and residents who pulled wheeled suitcases that dolled out *una cervaza por uno euro* and moved onto the next one who would be in need of the intoxicating distractions of this given modern life, unable to create for themselves the distractions that could so easily be found if we just looked. If we just looked at the absolutely intoxicating rhythms of the local Spaniards who at the end of the night in *Plaza del Castillo* danced in unison to the traditional flutes and snares piping out the songs of the land, the coordinated fashion that in circles around the centuries-old gazebo in the center of the square where the players played, the sounds sounded and the rays shone outward like a beacon to indicate to the dancers when to raise up, when to drop down, and when to circle one another like bees on the petal. How so many could at once be drawn to the music like flies to the light was a remarkable sight to see, and how so many knew so well the movements without instruction was also a stupendous thing to behold. To join in for a few minutes when the dance became a race, the partakers raising their bandanas as if to create a tunnel of bridges for others to pass through while the snare drum hissed like a snake, the sun downing now at half-past 10pm so late that the blue still seems deeply plush as it descends more and more over the plaza square now beaming with orange-tinted lights in a myriad of white bouncing over the golden tinted streets. Majestic, surely. Noble even, and in some ways of nobility. This is the nectar of the hedonist gods.

Separating the men from the gods at San Fermin were the bull fights. An honest to god bull fight, matador vs. *toro*. On this day I was repeating *ad nauseum* "I will not live my life in regret for having missed the bull run," and satiated a little bit of the remorse by attending the opening bull fight. Even that didn't seem real, and after having nearly been killed by what I thought was a bull in the ring, it peaked my interest what matrimony would unfold in the ring on this night. We found a ticket scalper during the day and set about preparing our minds and bodies until the doors of the arena would open (read: drinking). I purchased two 1-liter bottles of local San Miguel *birra* and walked to the gates.

Something here needs to be said of the casual nature of the Spanish. I am still unsure if it is owed to the nature of the festival or to the spirit of the Spanish people entire, but as I mentioned before I spent the festival shirtless. It was just more comfortable and often easier to clean since, as I've mentioned, wine was being tossed onto everyone all day and night. I had a cigarette burning in my mouth, large glass bottles of beer in each hand, and walked right up to the gate to hand over my ticket. I purchased a seat cushion and made my way up the stairs to the upper level looking like a mixture of unkempt homelessness, beach hair, covered in wine and tattoos, smoking and carrying open alcohol containers, dirt head to toe, and no one said anything or gave more than a glance in my direction. It was as easy as "*caul es la dirección*" and "*el asiento está arriba*" and there I sat in waiting. I understood this visual statement of mine to be unusual, even just slightly, but to seem as if it was completely acceptable at all times or even just during the bullfight, was quite bewildering.

We found our seats among the upper rows but were pleased to have good sight lines to the ring below and bit of shade. Reading earlier, I had learned that throughout the festival there existed cliques known as *peñas* in the festival which could be described as something of a fraternity that gathers once a year to organize music and parties for its members. The *peñas* battled each other throughout the day for notoriety, a battle that was always fought on the field of drunkenness. We knew they were entering the building when the marching bands started ringing throughout the halls of the arena, soon followed by the color-coordinated groups that wore distinctive hats and carried large signs for their publicity. Each member of a *peña* wore the ceremonial white, but instead of a red bandana might wear, say, blue for one whole group or green for another. I say all this because at the bullfights, their challenge of bravado is waged in the sun. Down on the first rows of the stadium situated on the eastern side where the sun bore down, it was there that they consumed heavy amounts of alcohol and danced to the traditional rhythms of the horn sections of their *peña*. In total there were about six *peñas* and three bands amongst them, all playing over each other. The beauty of it climaxed as the groups inflated balloons of their distinctive color and began to throw them into the air, creating a color wheel across the stadium sections left to right, a whole section of yellow balloons and a whole section of green balloons and a whole section of blue balloons, all dancing in the air.

But the real beauty had not yet begun. After the groundskeepers had finished raking and painting circles in the sand, the mayor took his seat at the grand stand as processional leader and in came *los matadores y los banderilleros y picadores*. The suits were as fantastic as any you may have seen in film or in cartoons, and every bit as bright in the evening sun. In turn they walked toward the mayor to take a bow, walking to one side and then another back toward their places where the matadors grabbed their capes and began to practice their *veronicas*. It took only a minute and the groundskeepers again came out to rake up quickly the footprints in the sand, leaving the ring empty. And without a sound or so much as a horn, the first bull came charging out into the ring.

The bull was huge. He stood to the shoulders of the matador and would charge from 15 meters out, chasing after the capes that were shook from side to side. In the early stages, the "first third" of the fight, the matadors would simply goad the bull toward their direction and against the wall, a team of three matadors working to get the bull to run from one side to the next. Occasionally one might get within a few feet but there were no passes, no *veronicas*. But as soon as we began to

147

wonder what would happen or when the fight would start, out came the *picadors*.

Picadors ride on a horse. The horse is covered in what looks like yellow leather sheets, strapped and tied from the top of the horse down its sides and wrapped under its stomach on all sides front and back. Its eyes are blindfolded and the *picador* carries a long spear. The spear is used to slice the bull's neck when it charges, because without failure the bull would immediately charge the horse. Worse yet, the bull would size the horse up and slowly turn its head to the side, plunging the horn first into the ribcage of the horse with such a force that the horse and rider would be lifted into the air. As the bull's horn got stuck in the side of the horse, the *picador* would reach down and stab the tuft of muscle atop the bull's neck until it would release. This must be done a minimum five times before the *picador* can exit the ring or the bull will be returned to the pen to be saved and the fight is over. But after the bull had been stabbed and finally released the horse, the *picador* slowly trotted the horse away that for as long as I could tell had no indication of what had happened to it, not making a noise. I learned later that it was only in 1935 after hundreds of years of fights, that it became. law to protect the horses with the shielding. Before then the horses were blindfolded and forced to take an almost certain fatal goring from the bull, and the *picador's* job to survive the ensuing scrum *and* wound the bull the appropriate times. That no longer being the case, the horse just walked away. Remarkable.

Into the "middle third" as the bull was a bit slower now and the *banderilleros* grabbed those sticks. I don't know what they're called but you have an idea of what I mean. The sticks that are about one-foot long and are striped with color, of which I learned indicate where the *banderillero* is from. Two matadors would guide the bull into the center of the ring where the *banderillero* stood with the hooked sticks.

It was like a coordinated ballet seeing their moves.

Coordinated ballet with a bull, but a pairing of which seemed nearer to art than slaughter. After the bull was guided into the center of the ring the *banderillero* would call for its attention by shouting and raising his arms at 45° angles, the hooks facing inward. In that position the *banderillero* resembled a striking snake, and in that position he would stand as the bull charged him full speed. Just as the bull approached he would begin to take just a single step or two to one side without turning, and just as the bull lowered his head to plunge forward the *banderillero* would jump and lean far enough over to stab the hooks deep into the open wound at the top of the bull's neck, dancing away unharmed to the roar of the crowd. This would happen at least three times until a total of six hooks hung from the wound atop its shoulders, its speed rapidly decreasing, its charges numbering fewer and fewer, provocation needed more and more to get the bull to attack. At its slowest speed now the matador would emerge.

The matador's entrance to the ring for the "death third" was like that of a painter approaching the canvas. His steps were smooth, the shoulders square and the object, the bull, square in his sights. And from only a few feet away from the bull the matador would reach out the cape to his side and lower it to the ground. When the cape just grazed the sand he would shake it violently, the bull charging head first at the moving object, the matador moving in a *veronica* to the side by merely rotating his hips, not taking a step in any direction.

It was, as they say, an art of the highest form. Like the tides rise and the currents move underneath, the music of this nature was iridescent in the shade of the arena, a transfixing waltz between matador and bull, man and animal, life and death. The blood flowed now along all sides of the bull, weakened to a point that even its rage seemed not enough to keep the will to survive in volatility. *¡Olé!* and to the side again, *¡olé!* and again turning, the bull charging, its movements in a circle around the matador that did not budge from his spot. The knees locked, his legs straight as trunks planted in the ground, only his shoulders whirring around and his sight changing from forward to backward as the beast circled his moves following the cape from front to back to front again until the matador would place the cape behind his legs and walk away from the bull, chest filled with air and chin pointed upward to goad from the crowd the swell of cheers that filled the space up to the sky, the bull left to pant and breathe heavily just to remain on its feet. Then the matador would return and this time walk right up to the horns. *¡Olé!* and rotate and *¡olé!* and spin and then stop with the cape behind his legs, the bull directly in feet, to begin to shake his legs back and forth asking the bull "would you care to dance?"

Such life at the hands of death. If the bull in this state just once thought to expend its energy both would be lost there in the sand, in the center for thousands to see. But the music went on, up and down there in the ring with no noise but loud enough for all to hear and see, this was the waltz that packed the house, this was the meal that served the multitudes, this is the art that will live on to be appreciated for generations to come because only a man tilted on equal parts genius and madness could manifest such magnificence and audacity, such equilibrium of living and dying. The barks of the matador could occasionally be heard, his calls the sirens of the living who were afraid not to die. *¡Olé!* and a turn *¡olé!* and the matador was away again to taunt the bull without so much as looking back because his gallantry had no limits, his acumen no threshold, his flare for the spectacular evinced in the daring dance of the dead performed by the living. I have never seen a man so alive before, and he was by all rights on the verge of death. There was one who got on his knees there before the bull. The matador got down maybe inches from the bull's horns and placed his eyes at the bull's level, on his knees with arms outstretched, walking on his knees back and forth. He looked as if in a vigil with the devil, and I couldn't tell if he was praying to survive or to be gored. It wouldn't have mattered either way.

The matador would eventually walk to the edge and exchange the blade by which he held the cape for a sharper sword, walking back to the bull. This time there would be no *veronica*, there would be no *iolé!* as he stood right before the bull with shoulders squared at each other. The matador raised the sword to his nose, pointing it outward at the bull, holding the cape just below and in front of his legs. With a single shake of the cape the bull would lower his head for the charge and there the matador would take one step to the side, lowering the sword into the wound and gouging downward with all his force until all of the meter-long blade was sunk into the bull's girth, only the handle remaining to be seen. Standing there now, spitting out chunks of its lungs and heart, it took seconds for the bull to lose its footing and drop to the ground, dead. The bull had been killed and the dance was over. A team of three horses came out and dragged the bloody carcass away leaving a trail of blood in the sand that would be raked haphazardly by the groundskeepers. And just as quickly as it ended out charged another bull and the ballet began again, this time from the top.

It went on this way for six fights, the matadors doing their part to raise the stakes each time, one *banderillero* making a fatal move and finding his skull under the bull's hooves, carried away to a fate no one could be sure of. There was never any sign or indication, no noise from the arena to indicate any kind of start or stop, any kind of grade the mayor may have made on the performance below, only the roars from the crowd for the matadors who danced with death on that day. Each performance would last about 30 minutes in total, and each one passed the same way from stage to stage as the bulls charged full of life into the first third, and by the "death third" had given its body up to sacrifice. The ritual is not unlike the Mayans who played games to determine who would live and who would die, the Egyptians sacrificing cow and lamb for rain, the Jews sacrificing lamb for eternity, the Romans sacrificing gladiators for spectacle, or any those of ancients who sacrificed their own to the gods. The gods in this spectacle were nameless, but the wages were the same as had been for thousands of years. Man needed death to be alive.

We woke up at 5am the next day having retired early after the fight. Missing the bull run was not an option, I repeat, missing the bull run was not an option. But even without *el encierro en la mañana,* my sentiment would have remained the same. The sobriety of the festival, seen now through the bullfights, was beginning to sink in. And as much as I wanted to dance my own way through the golden streets at night to be amongst the people, it was hard to feel at place with the celebrations going on, now knuckle-deep in the mire with fights each day.

Even as, Micah, Artur, and I walked within a few blocks of the arena by 6:15am we entered a running pace, in sync and at the same time without announcement as if we all felt the urgency equally. Being on the outside of the fence was unacceptable. I had come across the earth, flown over Europe, and driven across half of Spain *to run from those damn bulls and I was going to run from those bulls dammit.* I would not live a life in regret to have come so close and done nothing, to have gone so far and changed nothing in myself. I needed this more each minute.

When we saw the arena we saw also the fence and as Artur began looking for the gate I shouted, "just climb the fence, there, there!" and we jumped through the beams. Standing there inside the fences brought about a sense of relief. It was if I had arrived and in the hour-and-a-half between then and the start of the run I would let nobody remove me from the bull's way. We started walking down the route toward the beginning to get as much in the way as possible.

With everything we had learned and heard of the runs, we knew we needed to be somewhere on either side of *curva del muerte*, Dead Man's Curve. Dead Man's Curve took up the 50-meter space between two 90° turns, one left and one right, that formed an S-shape in the route starting at the town hall. It was Dead Man's Curve because a running formation of fighting bulls at full speed weren't the best at taking turns, instead smashing into walls and crushing whatever got in their way. Wisely we didn't want to be in that way, but the timing of avoiding it would take a bit of play.

The bulls were released in two groups of six. A firework would be fired to signal that the first bull of the first group was out of the pen, and a second firework would be fired to signal that the group had left the pen entirely. The same series of fireworks would be fired for the second group, usually about 20 to 30 seconds later. This meant that if I ran with the first group of bulls at town hall, before Dead Man's Curve, I would have to chase these bulls and get through the group of about 1,500 runners all the way through Dead Man's Curve and down the remaining 600 meters of road into the ring, all before the other group of bulls could catch me. I didn't see that as a likelihood and we decided to start after Dead Man's Curve. Avoid the whole thing entirely. I kept hearing the Irish lad in my head saying "dow'unt run the curve" and took his advice in whole. We would not be running the curve.

Other groups of Americans picked up on our voices, or maybe it was my suspenders and headband, or maybe it was nothing at all, but there formed a smattering of some 10 Americans all discussing the best ways to survive. None of us knew then the weight of the words we chose inadvertently, words like "not dying" and "surviving" and "running away" and "jumping for safety" that we callously tossed along as if we knew that those words should be taken as precisely as they are written – not to die on this day. But the groups all reached the same conclusions, even with a few who had run before. Monday's running group would be the largest of the festival and to avoid all issues, we'd start ahead of the curve.

Starting ahead of the curve did a few other things for us. It allowed us to get a chance at seeing the forces that were coming our way and allowed us to get into the ring before the second group of bulls could run us over. Of course all of this is theoretical, but we hoped its practice would executed the same way. But as the minutes waned we heard that the police would sweep the runners out of the road if they didn't start before Dead Man's Curve, to give the cleaners a chance to clear the road of any debris. So we watched in the middle of Dead Man's Curve as the police piled into the road and begin to take their spots along the fence. We felt we were safe enough until the most blessed man I've ever met approached me, and in broken English with a Spanish accent said, "if you want to run, you must start before the curve," and he pointed behind us. "The police will move you out, you must start there." He smiled and picked his camera up again to start taking pictures and all we could do was thank him before running into the large group of thousands that had found a way to smash into the alley between *Plaza Consistorial* and Dead Man's Curve. We jammed our way maybe a few feet into the group when the police on the other side where we had just run from began to sweep the crowds out of the road. What a blessing.

It was here that we waited to run, wondering if we would get the chance to spread out along the road once the sweeping was done, or if we would have to run the curve. It was also here that the most hilarious thing of the whole festival took place.

It's common throughout the festival to rent balconies for any number of the events that take place, so that tourists might get a better view of what's going on below during the runs, the parades, the street music, any time of day. Of course the runs are the most popular attraction, so as we stood there crammed into the mass of would-be runners, we had above us for each of about four levels up a household's worth of onlookers. On this morning directly above us stood a very attractive brunette woman of maybe 30-years old, turned slightly to the side as she spoke with whom I could presume was her mother. As the crowds began to cheer and whistle at her, she only laughed and looked up to the floor above thinking that we were not taunting her for wearing a skirt directly above us. Even as one man in the crowd with us began to point directly at her, blowing her kisses, as the crowd noise erupted in cheers and applause and shouts of *"eh punta"* she again kept looking up and laughing thinking that she was not the object of our affection. (If you're wondering, the panties were white, normal cut, no thong, but god she had beautiful legs) After five minutes or so, the man to her right turned to her and whispered in her ear while laughing. She entered the building and never came back.

With about ten minutes to go the runners were allowed to disperse along the route. We started our walk past Dead Man's Curve with no regrets for anyone that may call us pussies. I may go back one day and run Dead Man's Curve, but not on my first run. And just as we began to get past I saw the police gripping people by the neck and tossing them out. These were people holding up cameras. Strictly forbidden, it was being enforced by physically tossing people through the fence. As Artur came up to me with his camera and say "I'm glad I'm putting this away," he didn't put it away fast enough and got an arm around his throat until he was shoved through the fence. I stood there trying to goad him back, as I thought the police were not looking behind the fence to catch him if he jumped back, but did not. That left Micah and I to wander up the road to the hands of fate.

As we got about 50 meters past Dead Man's Curve we slowed to a stop. The impulse to keep going had filled us as hundreds of runners went walking past us closer to the arena, some slowly, some at a trot, some running. We were approaching three minutes to the fireworks to signal the start when people started running at full pace. I couldn't believe that so many people would be taking off ahead, but then, maybe I didn't know the depths of fear. Maybe this was only possible because I hadn't yet tapped the true bottoms of terror to know what I was doing. And as we moved to the side of the road that was maybe five meters wide, we watched the runners going by. I told Micah to stay nearer the middle of the road to avoid being pinned against the wall by other runners as the bull's passed, but a man overheard us and told us quickly, "no, get over here and let the chicken runners be the one's in the middle of the road when they come by" and I knew he was right. The people that were running now and the people that would freak out at the mere sight would be the ones to get run over, not me. And so I stood about a meter from the wall and waited.

I began to jump up and down and laugh, slapping my legs with the rolled up newspaper I was holding. I began to laugh and laugh and laugh more and more as the seconds ticked down and more people began to run by me. I couldn't help it, knowing that death in the form of horns would be running at me full speed. I had no idea what it would look like or how fast it would be but there I was anyway. And just then Micah remembered to watch the cameras. We couldn't see over the crowd of runners to know when the bulls would hit the corner, but we could see the television camera two floors up. When it turned, the bulls were turning.

That's when the firework went off. There were screams and people began sprinting up the road. The screaming went on as people shuffled by but through the noise Micah and I shouted "watch the camera! Watch the camera!" People were running at a faster rate now, the noise swelling almost to a deafening roar. The road was dark because the sun hadn't risen over, and staring at the camera in the sun at the end gave me tunnel vision. It was pointed out to the left but just then it dipped down to look just below and began to rise up in my direction. *Here they come.*

In that moment there is no fear. The time for fear has passed and I was left an alarming sensation of wonder, the kind of hyper-tensified alertness that strikes an animal in the wild. It became thoughts of "have I done enough?" and "what will they look like?" and "where do I go?" The thunder of noise rushed toward me and all I could see were the people, the white shirts and spots of red among it that formed a wall in the road racing my direction. I had no idea if the people were ahead of the bulls or not.

As the mass approached within five meters or so the people split rapidly toward the walls and without great focus I could see a huge brown and white boulder barreling toward me. The horns stuck out wide and straight from the skull of the bulls that were running down the street two bulls wide and three rows deep. Within less than a second they were on me and I did as I was told, as I had read, as I had heard: I hit the fucking wall. The people along the street did the same thing, but we all reached this conclusion more out of survival than any amount of preparation could allude. Having stood nearer to the middle of the road I was on the outside of the rows of people scratching for bricks to climb, myself nearest the bulls. I stood with my back to the people as if a man standing on the precipice of a cliff would keep his back to the rocks. I remember being shocked at that moment to learn that the bulls were outfitted with giant cowbells, and as they galloped by the noise became a mixture of giant hooves slamming against the ground like a thousand bass drums coupled with the booming CLONG CLONG CLONG CLONG CLONG of the cowbells, and as quickly as they had appeared the horns were racing by within maybe a half of a foot of my exposed torso, and then they were past me.

Survival kicked in again as I turned into the road to take off after the formation of animals. Though I had planned to follow them anyway, it felt in that moment, in that split second of time, that a decision had been made — I could wait here for the chaos to subside, but this chaos would proceed to the second formation of bulls. Better instincts took over.

Just as I did so immediately, so too did the other hundred or so people in my immediate area, all reaching the same conclusion at the same time, to *run fucking run*. As closely as we could to the tail of the bulls we poured out into the street to give chase, and it became apparent what the greatest danger was – other runners. By luck and chance my position nearest to the bulls away from the wall gave me the advantage of taking the first and clearest step into the street, finding a line in the middle to book it for all hell or find out how close the second bulls were. I hadn't taken a single step, the tails of the bulls almost within my reach when I saw the first of the runners to be pushed into the way of the storm, a man hitting the side of the bulls and going down to the ground, rolling into the fetal position as the 1200lb animals stomped and jumped over his body. In my peripherals I could see people struggling to get released from the crowd along the wall as they too tried to join the chase and we were left to jump over the mass of bodies that began to form along the road, some tossed to the ground by the feet of the bulls and many others thrown down by the people nearest them. Worse yet, the road was still slick from the alcohol that had rained down on the streets for two days and as we reached out with our legs to take each step it became a game of skill to stay on our feet, bystanders in our way notwithstanding. At about twenty paces as the street turned uphill I was forced to run on my toes to avoid going down, to keep from ending up on the ground under the feet of the runners and soon after the hooves of the second group of bulls. It was in this moment that I knew what the Irish man meant by "if you go dow'un, stay the fuck dow'un." There is no getting up in this heat. The few brave souls that tried to get up were immediately trampled again, and I thanked the ones who stayed down by jumping over their bodies further on toward the ring.

At about 250 meters, the route entered the intersection just before the arena, and though the fences we ran in didn't widen, the buildings outside the fence gave way to open space. People here were able to sit along the fences that we ran inside, and it felt like celebrating a victory as the voices cheered. The need to laugh overcame me and for whatever reason I turned around to run backward and see for once the mess I was in. It was beautiful. I could only take a few steps before other people were running into me, forcing me to turn back around. But in those seconds I felt like I was in the presence of the Lord, the entire spirit of the human race unfolded before me, the universe collapsed here and started again with the fever pitch of death. We had run. Or were running, as we came upon the entrance to the ring. Down the slope and I was into the arena full of spectators, the noise and ambience of which made me feel like an Olympic champion taking the platform. Dashing off to the right I turned around and not five seconds behind me the crowd split, with a group just at the entrance to the ring all hitting the ground – the second group of bulls were jumping over these people into the ring and with as much speed as the ones I had passed were across the 100 meters of the ring within a second's time to be corralled in their pen at the end. It became a sea of joy in that building.

The ritual had only just begun and soon enough the oxen were released one by one as they had been the day before, in fact it was the same oxen as before. The brown one with the lopsided pair of horns coming out first. Attempting to give him chase I learned immediately that the number of people in the ring on this second day easily tripled the amount of the first. On the day before when I was nearly pummeled by an ox there were spaces along the wall to jump, the crowd not so thick you couldn't get a look at it before it speared your way. But on this day there were no spaces. The people were lining the walls so heavily that to get out demanded great inconsequence, and seemed nearly impossible. And as the first ox left the ring after a few minutes, I learned that his replacement was the bastard that nearly killed me. That big, black, hulking mass of anger was back out in the ring. I made one attempt to get at him and very nearly got thrown to the ground by the people around me. So many in fact that it was impossible to make a move toward the beast. Instead people were just standing around waiting for him to approach, their only guesses of his movement were the people spreading to one side and then the next and often that indication was inaccurate. I feared more greatly in that crowd than I had at any moment. Panic overwhelmed me that I couldn't see the thing that wanted me dead, nor could I escape. I started running along the walls until I came to the matador's exit, pushing my way through against the weight of the revelers there watching. I found a small patch of wall to look out and made peace that I had survived. It would be enough to watch the rest from safety.

For the next hour a few more oxen were released one by one. The runners in the ring were a mixture of people who knew what was going on, and people who didn't. From the size of the crowd it was probably more of the latter. The English-speaking tourists who would stop inside the ring to take pictures with each other while the ox kept fucking raging around. It was a sport to see which runners would not realize that it was coming in their direction, and the reactions they made. Most immediately jumped for the wall, but given on this day the amount of people keeping escape closed, the runners would instead just jump in our arms. It went on like this until *el encierro* had finished and the people began pouring out into the streets.

They took with them a bit of life. At least that's what they gave me. The tingling that super-whelmed my body the last time showed up again this morning, but it brought along with it relief. The sun seemed a bit brighter, but only as exit music for a trio of non-heroes. We weren't anything spectacular. We had merely run.

It didn't feel real in some ways. To swim the ether from the goddamned bottom wells of fear, fear so deep that a calm cleanses the senses, up to the very mountains of oblivion and life so rich that the feeling of immortality must be swatted from the face like flies. I was nearly frozen in the Spanish heat. The steps guided me home but the heart raced along as if the run had never ended. The spirit soared to gain witness over the city entire with its millions running mad, mad they ran into the third day like the first had never ended, God had instead said that the first day will be extended first to 48 hours then to 72 hours then infinity as the streets entered the rain cycle from dry to soaked, a heavy precipitation of booze and filth poured down at interval hours when the drunks weren't eating. I'm sure that no one slept on these days.

To sleep would be asking too much. The things we'd miss in sleep would deprive the barren spirit inside the bones. How could I be expected to see around me so much life and say to it that I would not also? We were here to drink rich in the waters of life welling from the springs of death, that was the play. The play that death could deal for us so much life. That for the bulls, that for the runs, that for the fights, that for the brazen intoxication that could last for days, that for these things we would be rewarded with a cosmic breath lasting unto forever. Untold wealth filled the pockets of the poorest of men in these days. It's a shame then that it must end, but I believe it ends because we let it. This could go on forever if so many wanted to be so rich, if so many would give up on running from death and just jump out in front to see if it would race by or gore them with horns. The life that does so is not without a purpose. It is balanced. It is about both living and dying. To deny death is to deny life. And so we run.

Which way do you run?

Before Me Lied a New Dawn

Before me lied a new dawn. It came in the form of green, rolling hills shaded orange as a clementine from the rising sun, dotted with dark tones from the line of trees just on the horizon, a bit of brush lining the creeks at the lowest point. I had just filled my bag with a collection of the local lagers and *Trappistes*, enough to make merry myself and the few soldiers that marched along. We hadn't made it fifty meters down the trail before I stopped in a moment of clarity seen before only in the tales of Christ and Crusoe: this would be a new way forward.

Clarity there existed in the folding iron fence taken over by the grips of time. Only a single cemented post remained upright, a half-rolled distance of chicken-wire pulling out from one side before stopping not at its destination but upon an indeterminate length of grass, the total of which enclosed nothing. The cemented post was adorned with the artisanal etching of a rooster, as sure as the chicken that now clucked its way down the slow hill toward the faint amount of water nestled in the crest of the valley. The valley of which rolled back up and over again and down and around on all sides like the bubbling sheets of water that move over a creek bed of rocks, themselves smoothed over with the washing of time. This was Bastogne, Belgium. The scene was lifted straight from a film or a history book, and the image was modern, timeless, and iconic all at once. It looked like the last relics of the great war.

This was my first major trip since arriving in Germany and I wasn't prepared. Only the night before we had arrived at the township where we would stay, LaRoche en Ardennes, a 25-kilometer jaunt through the rising hills-turned-mountains that we couldn't see because of our nighttime drive. What I could see when we entered the city in darkness was the white river below the only street of the town, lit from the bulbs that illuminated its presence there in the village, a way for the residents to announce and honor the heart of their little town. It seemed necessary to light it as a warning because of the sharp cliff walls that rose on either side as we drove toward the hotel pushing travelers to the waterline, and when we parked and exited the vehicles I could hear from all sides, all angles around me the *hissssss* of the water as it passed quickly over the rocks. The sound echoed off the rock walls and seemed to be coming from all corners, though I learned in reality a few short minutes later that it came from a river not even 20-centimeters deep, the water clear as day and moving fast like the wind. There was not a single shrub or sandbar to stand in its way, only the multitude of rocks and stones that made for the water its tambourine to play. I hadn't even seen the mountains or hills yet and already I knew things were changing.

As the sun came over the hills that next morning when I stumbled onto the scene of the fence, as the world opened itself to me, I learned then that certain things were imminently more important than my own triviality. We were there to celebrate and commemorate the liberation of the Ardennes by the Allied Forces at a place and during a time remembered in America as the *Battle of the Bulge* for the bulging appearance of the offensive front line drawn on a map, or by Germans as *Unternehmen Wacht am Rhein*, "Operation Watch on the Rhein," or more simply as the French call it *Bataille des Ardennes*, "Battle of the Ardennes." We were told to go in uniform, to march in uniform, and (for my own purposes) to drink in uniform, that all and sundry would be doing the same. "Everyone's going to be in some kind of uniform and marching along," I'd heard. I didn't know that it would be an entire city and valley full of persons in costume, a veritable army-sized element of patrons in the full regalia of the German SS and another half decked out in the uniforms of the Allied American forces, complete with 101st Airborne Division patches, the Screamin' Eagles. The tanks sat on the edge of town, the forest-green motorcycles whirred by with troops riding in sidecars, Jeeps filled the streets and all around were the sounds of joy and cheer erupting from the residents, the revelers, and the soldiers, one and each united in a reverie equal to the transmogrification of souls. *We were nearer to heaven.*

Total and complete strangers were best friends meeting in the streets, the alleys, the muddied, foot-trodden paths from farm to farm outside the town where the march went along. Stories of battles, fables of relatives who fought, invitations to trade pictures and gear and patches and souvenirs and drinks, the many drinks. And where language wasn't enough, we'd shuffle and dance the language of our ancestors until the meaning was understood. The language was probably better then, after all. People came together. I had reason to feel a part of something, rather than as a spectator.

For all the things I've done to this point in my life, it was as if I were watching a show unfold before me. And taking then the memories of those events past, the end result is what? The accumulation of experiences as memories, as events I've witnessed to be logged, categorized, and set upon like a trophy to dignify a life deemed lived. "Indeed, the true adventurer must come to realize, long before he has come to the end of his wanderings, that there is something stupid about the mere accumulation of wonderful experiences," as Miller says. This had been the way of life, the modern American living. Justly it means predilection, predictability, sooth-saying for the masses. We are set about in a world that has been meticulously charted, categorized, and defined in such and so many delicate patterns, void of embarrassment, danger, and consistent with sterility and sanitation that to row about its waters is merely to navigate the Antietam during a drought. What then? Is it so difficult then to obtain employment in a nation filled with employers and employees? No. The details may change, but derivation from the mean is nil. Think then of all the events encompassing the greater moments of your life and realize, how abstract and void of bravado we have been – graduating high school, then college, playing sports and attending concerts, getting married and having children. All of these earmarks to our outstanding existence come hedged with no bets.

A few weeks after returning from Bastogne I was in Rome. *Roma, Italia, of Lazio.* Wine soaked. Wine *flooded.* For five days I operated in the hazy confines of a swimming pool above ground, seeing things with one eye closed. It was New Year's and Italian wine was served 5€ to the bottle, a price for something so exquisite I got the bargain by drinking the city's proper share. If you had locked me up into Amontillado's cask I'd have said good riddance. And this was for all its good because I was not alone. There in a city of a couple million came down a few more million, something that surprised me but what I should've expected. And in all, there were but a few recourses for the days and nights – to see and imbibe all at once and without end the beauty of the Eternal City. Without sleep and without rest and without ceasing, there as the sun rose and made way to moonlit empty villas, was a city drunk on spirits, of both the fermented and mystical kind. Where in Bastogne I had been enveloped in an era, tucked away into a time of being as if a vacuum had pulled me directly into 1945, Rome had placed me within a bubble. For the first time I could focus on the knowledge that *history as I know it is mine and mine alone.* Nothing about what the Romans built and accomplished some two- and three-thousand years before had bearing on my behavior in that moment, and it was beautiful.

I didn't go there expecting any one thing. I wasn't trying to raise Caesar's ghost or channel Marcus Aurelius and didn't think to impress Constantine. Their histories created the city as it was in their own time, like the millions of cities around the world that have each their founders, but these cities do not persist because of these ancient heroes. The cities persist because of the people, and for five days I was a citizen of Rome. I did my best to be a modern Roman – morning for pasta and wine, a *birra* walking the stone way surrounding the Coliseum, grilled eggplant and wine for lunch, a foot tour of the Pantheon and a bottle of wine by the Fontana di Trevi, and the night into Campo de Fiori, drinks in hand, football kicked through the square, music playing in all corners, fireworks thrown up into the air, and later, late when each boy and girl have tucked away in bed or asleep on the ground and the streets are empty, there I embarked to see the city at night. It was like seeing a ghost. Nothing could successfully describe the effect of removing at night the millions of people present by day. Like standing in the empty stadium lit only by moonlight – where thousands just earlier gathered now sat not even electricity.

But it was all so fluid and tangible, so very real. I didn't meet anyone on that voyage into the heart of Rome but I never felt disconnected. I was for the first time a part of something, as I was in Bastogne. I wasn't just a fish in a sea full of sharks, but a member of a school. Each of us independent but linked, moving in succession. I saw the greater works of the things before me, of me, after me, the depths of the human spirit equaled by its imagination. And for all the things we've done and continue to do that keep us from moving forward, the simple moments of splendor often remain as the most serene. Getting drunk seems so naïve, but drinking with a few million of your new best friends can be euphoric. I'll always remember being in a crowd so thick that I was lifted up by the weight of the people around me, thousands in the middle of the Forum Romana, a backdrop of a glowing Coliseum, a white-lit Arc di Constantinople, ahead the golden Capitale.

Each day like that was built upon the predilection that anything truly was possible. The rest of the year for me, before being trapped in the desert for nine months of a deployment, was an experiment in time and possibility. The experiment was where and how, the possibility as always – *women.*

Could never be sure when or where but in the back of my mind always is a woman. Not one, though sometimes, but always all in general. The savagery of such notion is absurd. Desire for romance is just too strong to be anything less than the primal urge.

So put me then into a world unknown and leave inside me the pursuit of women, of romance, of raw sex. I felt like Sir Edmund Hillary crossing the icy poles. I knew what would be out there, but not how to get it, to hold it, in what its forms would be. This made the tender evenings *sparkle* with possibilities. Over those few months I spent three consecutive days in the sewers of the Carnivale abyss, drenched in the beer and liquor and wine that seemingly fell from the sky during German *Fasching*, a Mardi Gras to end them all. I discovered the beauty of the Czech *laissez faire*, the sheer fuck-all way of life that gripped a nation formerly torn of war and made for it the simplicity of a group of friends in a bar to be the highest nobility. I learned that Easter Sunday was not too sacred for sex in a club bathroom stall. I learned to dance, rather, to become absorbed by music in a club, to swing and sway and let roll my head there on the floor and become only the body moving in the crowd, high on as much ecstasy in its divine form as in its narcotic form, in only the ways a seedy underground Czech club can make it so. I learned to care so little about the atmosphere that, placed in the middle of the woods and with no one around, I could achieve the same effect given the right music and the right woman. And I learned that sometimes never seeing someone again isn't always never.

I learned also that I could do all this alone and for myself. I *needed* to do all this alone and for myself. No one could tell me the right ways to fly across the planet to see about a girl, because there is no right way and I couldn't have been wrong at all because I tried. No one could make it easier to walk the streets of Helsinki cold and alone looking for a hotel and having, in a world and a language as foreign as fire to the Neanderthal, to speak up and ask for help. No one opens my mouth in those moments and says for me the words that come out. No one made for me the friends I have all over the world, no one created for me the scenarios in which I operated and drank and fucked and danced and swam and sang and drew out the sweet nectar of life by seeing just seeing that all those pictures aren't pictures, they aren't the real thing, the real thing is there wherever it is waiting to be seen or held like the mighty Neva river rolling through the middle of St. Petersburg because it can't be told or written or seen in a picture how cold the wind feels off the sheet of ice covering its dark waters during the Russian Christmas. I know what it smells like in the Sistine Chapel and I know what it feels like to stumble down the muddy hill to Gunpowder Pub and I know what it feels like to wake up in the snow and I know what it looks like to see the first Christmas tree in Riga and I know what it means to die as the bulls go running by in Pamplona, but I can't tell you these things. These things are infinitely possible, but they live in me as I experienced them. The history of these stories and these ideas cannot change inside me and likely have no power elsewhere. So go the best laid plans of the lunatic.

This new way forward unfolded before me as a result of my *tabula rosa* – I simply didn't know what to expect. I greeted everything with the rosy fondness of a puppy. The nights around were each and all unique in their ways, down even to the women and their languages and the clothes they wore. It was beautiful to guess the way nationalities would look, the predominant hair colors, the hoppiness of the beer, the strength of the coffee, the chances that she would speak English. It was all too much too often and every day then became a chance at something new. When it wasn't new anymore it broke my heart.

Coming back from nine months in the desert I tried to do it all over again. Every day was a sensational grab at the feelings I had created. Where I had before sat on the banks of the Gulf of Finland at 10pm and had yet to see the sun reach the horizon, watching the ice float across the water in mid-April and see the way the light bounced off the water and onto the clean white walls of Helsinki's buildings, there I had been birthed. Born again for a new way of seeing. Such a magnificent moment that now in its absence sat a life unfulfilled. As if every moment of my being had led to those moments, those moments walking the pasture hills of the south German farmland, the moments walking along the Salzach, drinking a Stiegl, dreaming of Mozart, and staring at the women walking over the *Markartsteg*, the moments taking shots from the beer cart in the middle of a street filled with Scooby-Doos, pilots, firefighters, pirates, Snow Whites, and fairies all at once drinking and dancing as the parade goes by, the moments getting jerked off on the outside patios of an upstairs club, the moments trying just to hold someone's hand walking through Töömemagi, or the moments spent idly, doing nothing, just sitting and watching the sun go down over the high-rise of old buildings, half-liter of *weißen* in hand. A fool's errand to chase these again.

A quote that has always stuck with me came from Norman Mailer – "the only faithfulness people have is toward emotions they're trying to recreate." The world of the sights and sounds I had seen before living in Kuwait became more like gold the further removed in time it sank, and like any fool I wanted to do it all over again. What I didn't realize, and still struggle with, is that it isn't possible.

There have been new beginnings, new possibilities, no mistake. But these new possibilities must be constructed in new ways, repeatedly and forever.

I couldn't go out there alone anymore. I came back from that desert and went into a new world, but I wasn't alone. I went to Riga and watched the world's oldest Christmas tree celebration, but I wasn't alone. I spent five days in a basement apartment drinking wine and building fires, but I wasn't alone. I walked along the Pilsêtas Kanal and fed the ducks who slid down the ice for a piece of bread, but I wasn't alone. And those moments not alone were magical. In their own way it was possible again to get that new, infinite feeling, because I wasn't doing it the same way as before. The feelings of joy and serendipity were linked to newness and to difference and change.

Some weeks after being there in Latvia and finding reinvigoration I was in Slovenia. The cold, forested, mountainous nation of Slovenia would be a winter trip for winter's sake. Friends of mine organized the journey to find the slopes, but I went to find the snow. Snow, and by that I mean to walk and be there in the mountains, to hike and be alone, to think and ponder and figure out where the year would be ahead. Slovenia became the first trip I would go on to signify how the year would go, as all the events just before had been a celebration of leaving the desert. This now, Slovenia, would be just life as I was living.

It was beautiful, make no mistake. Mountains as high and as steep as these I had never seen before. Coming through the slopes in Austria I woke on the bus to a scene truly picaresque – the cliffs of the mountains nearly straight up on all sides and in all directions, a sheer rock face of grey and black too steep to hold snow at any height, high up further than the eye would allow before being blocked by clouds, for miles and miles and miles and then, finally, just finally, the clouds break and from behind pours out the bluest sky with the brightest sun, there just behind at all times and waiting to be seen. It seemed as though the sun were always hiding this high up, or else it would not be so ready to make light with just a single break in the cloud line. Otherwise I suppose there would be more grey, but we were as high as the airplanes that break the cloud line on takeoff.

The snow was everywhere. It was so thick that I couldn't venture off trail to see anything other than the city where we camped. Our hotel was on the other side of the main lake in the town of Bled, and it became very apparent that the city existed on tourism and bypassers, a place to see with not much to offer when the timing wasn't right. Everywhere there pointed wooden arrows with distances indicating the paths to take to certain peaks, but with snow so deep that I'd be up to my knees, and it wasn't in the cards for me to disappear, should I not want to disappear terminally. So instead I walked the city streets and spent the days and evenings with my legs draped there over the walls of the castle that sat atop the mountain overlooking the lake and town below, the only hike made possible by the carved stone walkways on both sides. Evenings were spent in the same bar, writing some, reading some, passing time and staring out wondering what could have been, what I could've done, what should've happened, and thinking of god knows what. If I had put my mind together I'd have seen it for what it was, the year ahead.

A few weeks later it was Dresden, and a few weeks after that it was Nurnberg again. In no time it was Würzburg every weekend, and I couldn't figure out where the possibilities had gone. The more disappointment I found the harder I tried to recreate the circumstances by which I found it. If this bar didn't work then another might, or if this city didn't have it then surely another would.

What I never realized was that the possibilities were in me. They emanated from me outward and created the way forward. Where I deviated from the path I created for myself unhappiness, depression, no possibilities. I lost that *tabula rosa* – I let the things I learned about Europe, about the people, the food, the wine, the drinking and dancing and way of living dictate my behavior and at each one a dead end. The truth was still out there, but maybe it wasn't truth anymore that I needed.

So I wandered through Europe as if it were a desert, lost and un-seeking of anything. Just theeeerrrrrrreeeee... just there. Drifting.

I found it again. A couple of times it was there. Just as the sun had risen on that Belgian morning to tell me I was living, that feeling that shook my bones, it came back to me.

It was there on top the mountains of Sardegna, overlooking the Mediterranean Sea. There in just a few moments the winter broke to spring broke to summer and from a peak of maybe 300-meters up we looked down from the centuries-old tower to see below the beaches of Porto Ferro, lapped up again and again by the icy, dark waters coming in from the west, the sun falling below the horizon, that line so straight and wide and unending that our vision could follow it to the ends of the earth if Copernicus weren't so right. All the colors blended perfectly from the highest deep sea blue point in the starry night sky to the bright orange dot still sitting there in the middle of sight, laid out over the now black waters with rippling white lines flowing out and past us, the low, buzzing sound of the waves moving by with the wind and nothing but a straight drop down all the way to the rocks below.

It was there again that first night in Pamplona. We hadn't even run from the bulls yet, had only been in the city for an hour or so, had barely put our bags in the room before the excitement overwhelmed us and we set out on foot for no direction particular. In short we came across the town hall, the center of the festival, the signal of the event, picture of the city, the place that from its position outward came all the stories and images of the revelers in white running to and from and with the bulls so large and horned and carrying death and with it carrying life. The Town Hall is a building so magnificent that it was instantly recognizable as we came across at first by accident. There in a square foyer no larger than 70 meters by 25 meters rose the four-story building, possibly 20 meters wide, but straight out of the ground like a grand sequoia, and every bit as austere. Each level ordained with a magnificent amount of artisanship, the middle floor lined with all the flags of the Basque Country and Spain itself, orange from the ages of dust and sand and dirt and time that have passed at its feet, black all around from the dark, still Spanish night.

One week later I began a 160-kilometer foot march in the Netherlands, and there I found the feeling, too. The world's oldest and largest organized foot march, the *Vierdaagse*, or Four Days March. There were over 40,000 people participating in the grueling march, 40 kilometers (25 miles) a day, and over 100,000 people each day lining the streets to cheer us on, and every one of them with a beautiful story and a more beautiful smile. I have never in my life seen the kindness of humanity come forth so much as on the routes of that march, as thousands joined together to encourage one another to finish line. On those days it felt good to be a human being.

These things brought the feeling back to me because of the gravity of their existence. Either too beautiful, too important, or too alive to be neglected. It made me feel alive. It made me feel unimportant in the best way. It made me see the earth, it made me see the planet, it made me see the things out there other than my own problems. It made me feel like the last man, like the only one with the secret. It made me glad to be alive and to be a human being. It made me feel like the infinite was still possible. It made me see the ending and the beginning. It made me feel love, it made me feel hate. It made me see the darkness and the light and it made me happy for both. It made me regret nothing behind and be hopeful for everything ahead. These moments made me feel as the traveler charting new lands, standing on the pillars of the mountains overlooking the valleys below where no man has gone before, trodden with the antelope and deer and the bear and the moose and the lizards and the owls and the ox and the parrots and the spiders and the ants and all the things that for no good reason sprang up from the muck of the fire of the rock of this universe and for no good reason persist in spite of all forces against. Belgium in the sun, Rome at night, Helsinki by the water, Pamplona with its bulls, Sardegna over the sea, the plains of the Netherlands, these places, these places, these places at once and infinitely possessing of all the beauty and the possibilities in the world that for just a few minutes at a time I could live forever.

But there have been places that for these same reasons are empty. There in Paris I nearly got the feeling – Paris is a city of outstanding amazement, a true achievement in human creativity. But the people made the city in all its splendor, and they've since forsaken it. It left me as it is, empty. And that was the end of it.

I landed in Atlanta a few weeks after that.

Part III

EXIT THOUGHTS

April 2014 – August 2015

Where Do The Words Go?

Where do the words go?
Softly
Softly to the wind
Blown through the trees
And never heard again.
But such a sweet end -
Alone, quiet,
Surrounded by friends.
Other souls long too unused.
There also by way
Of neglect:
Laughter, poetry, strong cups of coffee
Between conversations about
Where does it all go?
And when you run your hands softly
Over the tops of the grass,
Cool, light, inviting, a shade of pleasant
But something true and cordial with Father Time,
Looking down then you will see where it all goes
And I wonder, oh, I wonder
When we will pick it back up.

Coffee

All I can think of is coffee
Kaffee, café, kohv, кофе
With milk, sometimes sugar
Sometimes cold (rarely).
Like mine black,
Nothing added.

Maybe a cigarette.
Always a cigarette.
And away goes the static.

/Crackling plastic, sifting grain, running water,
click and then sizzling, drop drop drop/

In the cup, steam rising
So damn warm,
Smooth roasted, no filter
And then!

Espresso, cappuccino, latte
Yes please
Just give me the caffeine
And a little time to think.

Evolving

Cleaning out is fine
Gone are the smokes, gone with meat,
Drinks, free sex.
It is cleaning, I am clean
But what next?
It feels, feels like a step out and on and upward
But who am I to leave humanity behind?

I am the dirty streets
I am the filthy sheets
I am the wild, naked and raging
Am the towers overhead
Am the dying and the dead
I am the whores
The corrupt
The smoke filling up
I am oh I am the graves
The trash blowing away
The sirens
Food stamps
Empty news stands
Yes, I am.

Tell me I am, I don't
Want to get so far that I lose touch and become some saint,
Discarded for grace
Better to make change
By sleeping with the _____.
Even 2000 years ago Jesus hung from the plank.

Unique Skillsets

I have unique skillsets. I have marketable characteristics. I have varied and useful experience, and the requisite bullet points. I have spent time in good places to spend time. I have an excellent education and a couple of degrees. I have no use for these.

I have colorful résumés. There's a green one, and a blue one. I have everything in line and powerful references. They're nice people who do nice things. I have the right attitude, and I'm approachable. I'd rather be far, far away.

I have many years ahead of me. I have potential for growth. I have one step on the ladder, and each step is a little more time. I have the ability to start at the bottom, and I have the strength to work to the top. I never do.

I have multiple outlets and many contacts. I have a broad network. I have places I could be, and people who want me. I have no need to try them again.

I have a lot of tools. I have endorsements and I have a track record. I have certifications and I have good training. I spend my time working on anything else.

I have a large collection of vinyl records. It's nice. I have an expensive stereo that plays the music and an expensive turntable that spins the wax. It's been my only dream, to own all the music. But it won't fit in my car when I need to leave.

I have a full closet. There's more than five jackets, a row of quality jeans, and a handful of vintage cloth. The shelf in the center holds my new felt hat, the kind that travellers wear on the train. It'll go with me when everything else gets thrown away.

I have a curated library. Nothing but the classics. Anyone could walk in and find something to read. Hardbacks and paperbacks, each chosen for the classic appeal, especially the ones with yellow pages. I'll put my favorite in my back pocket and the rest go to charity.

I have furniture. I have a bed, two sofas, and a coffee table. I never wanted furniture and never thought about buying it until I rented an apartment. I never considered what color, what type of wood, or what size. I never thought I needed furniture. I needed furniture when I wanted to be comfortable in the place I was living. I never thought of how much time could go by on a sofa I didn't need.

And now it's one more thing that won't fit in my car.

I have decorated with things that I enjoy. I put up canvases of places I've been, moments I've been happy, snapshots and pieces of memorabilia from where I've gone and want to go again. Postcards and concert posters and a collage of photos that help me remember. It was supposed to make me happy again. It only fills me with the worst kind of desire.

I have a nice, big bed. I have a mattress. A mattress is another thing I didn't think about, until I did. Again, the thinking was I needed a mattress. But a place to sleep isn't necessarily a mattress.

I have, over time, given away most all the rest. Childhood nostalgia, photo albums, unwanted and unread books, knick-knacks, unseasonable clothes, trinkets, outdated software, relics of hobbies I never finished, unworn shoes, framed pictures, anything that I couldn't take with me. Somehow I've gotten more. Each time I get something new, I try to give something away. The things that don't need to stay will really surprise you when you operate this way.

I still have too much.

I have little problems. The kind that seem monstrous to most, but really, I mean really really really, aren't worth my dime's bit of time and toil. I have an idea of who I want to be and no way of getting there, that's a bigger problem. The rest is *c'est la vie*.

I have places I want to go, things I want to do. I have ideas and creativities and arts all rolling around in my head, but I don't have the whatever-it-is to get after it. Instead I have a job, and furniture, and unique skills that get in the way.

I have no reason to worry. I have been in better places, but I have been in worse. I have no idea what's going to happen next, but I haven't been overcome yet with fear. I have things I could do, but I have only one that I want.

I want to choose. I want to be free. I want to have attorney over my soul. I want to move about, and be laughed at for dancing. I want never again to hide who I am.

All these things I have now I have because I've been hiding from myself. I won't have them much longer.

The Dust In a Line

There, to the east from the mountain
The dust in a line rises
From ants marching
Rolling in all terrain vehicles
Rolling in armored tanks
Rolling out to the field
Marching to victory.
All in a row
All without question
The call is "follow me!"

Where the desert winds pick the sand
Off the floor and through the air
It soars, clouding vision.
A fitting description.
But there also to the east is earth untouched,
Holes in the ground dug once but abandoned,
No more money, you see?
Now just empty mines
Though empty depends on your frame of mind.

To the ants
The money is the making
The money is in the march
The money is in the order
To follow someone to victory.

But in such desert, lonely places
Where high noon is all day

No shade from no tree
There in the mines away from the ants
I hide.
A cool wind drifts off the rocks.
That is not my army any longer.
That is not my war anymore.

Retrospective on a Weekend

It's been five years, two months, and two weeks since I believed in God, give or take a couple of days. For all the significant moments in my life that I remember exactly, I can't actually tell you which specific day it was, but I can remember that it was in the first two weeks of March of four years ago. It was a period of my life where all the days kind of run together, and I didn't have any reason then to treat a Sunday differently from a Wednesday differently from a Friday. But I woke up that morning, and as I've alluded to before, nothing peculiar happened. It was innocuous, the sky was the grey, the trees were blowing in the wind, and I looked up and felt that I was the only one responsible for my life. It was empowering. But I'm not here to tell you what I don't believe in. I want to spend a few minutes talking about the things I do believe in, and how last week I felt them again in many ways all at once. I feel rejuvenated.

I believe in the sanctity of human power. I believe that our evolution has set us apart for a reason, and we haven't found out the reason yet. I believe that our only steps forward will be harmonizing with the earth and our past. I believe that we can each do this individually, and should do this individually before we can ever hope for a better future as a planet and a biosphere at large. I wish I could swat a wand and change it all instantly, but I can't. Instead I evolve in my own way, and in these past few months and short years, I've done that by returning to nature, and for the first time have started to embrace this united nation as a frontier, the true limits of earth that it really is. And last week was the most holy I've felt in years.

Since coming back to America, I've been through the Appalachian Trail, up the waterfalls of Jefferson Forest, to the summit of Guadalupe Mountain, across the entire Chisos Basin in the Big Bend Mountains, seen the relics of Pueblo life carved into the Gila Wildnerness, been snowed in at the top of Lincoln National Forest, and will soon be embarking on my third trip into the Grand Canyon. It will be my first trip to the Colorado River though, and every time I'm reminded that it is sincerely the most spectacular land feature this rock of earth has ever created. But last week I nearly touched the heavens in a place called Chiricahua National Monument in the southeastern basin of Arizona.

Nothing can prepare a man for the moments of surprise only nature can create, because seeing truly is believing. I knew through reading that the monument was a relatively small, 100-acre-or-so area up the Coronado Wilderness, preserved for its unique rock formations. Some 100-million years ago Sugarloaf Mountain was an active volcano that erupted for the final time, spewing volcanic ash all throughout the basin. The ash-flows changed the rocks there into a supple Rhyolite, which over the last 100-million years has been eroded to create standing pillars of rock, each looming up from the ground to make shadows like giants. And from on top of any one of the pillars looking into Echo Canyon, it can seem like a buried army. It can seem like a place untouched, and for that it evokes the spirit of the holy.

More importantly, it is a stern reminder to me that there is a certain beauty that will always exist within the world no matter how hard the darkness of humanity casts over the land. My experiences here in America will be for the foreseeable future always marked by my impressions of my own past, my impressions of the different continents I've seen, and primarily the differences in the people I've met along the way. I did not want to return to America, and hiking there in Chiricahua I made the remark once, "such a beautiful land spoiled on such loathsome folk." It's a bit hyperbole, but it's a bit truth as well. Luckily I was in the presence of one of the most inspiring persons I know, and she was receptive to hear me ramble. This was something I hadn't been afforded in quite some time, but it allowed me to vocalize an idea I've been tossing around for a few weeks now.

Recognizing that the escape to nature is Muir-ian in it's own right, I couldn't help but wonder what facilitated such a transformation in myself. After having spent countless weekends wandering the sidewalks of any European city and wanting nothing but for coffee and conversation, how now did I revert to such apparent lonely desolation high in the mountaintops? Where did I decide I no longer wanted to be among the people of this world? It is, obviously, provoked by the people I am surrounded by. And it got me thinking about freedom.

We'll never be free, truly, I've given up on this. But there is a freedom to be found in different ways, individually. But this freedom here, this freedom in America as I've found it, comes with a price. The books will read and the films will show and the explorers will say, "there is freedom in the mountains," and they are right in some ways. But no matter how many hills I climb and how far away I get from the city, there will always be the underlying purpose that *I'm doing this to escape.* If I disappear into Yosemite never to return, even fifty years from now after spending every new day of my life there, I cannot forego the recognition that the freedom of that life is chained by the notion of having fled. And no matter how gratifying such a freedom can be, it is to me not honest. I had that honesty in the past, and it wasn't in America. In places of happiness, freedom existed because I utterly felt no compulsion to lead in any direction – there was an ostensible feeling that the end of any day would lead to bliss. And it didn't matter what I did. Most of my days were spent walking without a map and I always ended up exactly where I wanted to be, even if I didn't know where I was going. But here in this country, my escapes are always calculated. I enjoy them for their refreshing qualities, but their limitations are equally heartbreaking.

Finding the holiness then, is the thing to hold onto. I can

remember after a day of hiking while obscenely drunk, we ended in the Heart of Rocks, appropriately named. It is the south side of Echo Canyon and follows a draw out into the canyon, mazing through the giant figures above until resting on the edge of a cliff, staring out across the canyon with the sun setting over the range in the distance. We had a long conversation there about the things humans do to each other, and I became unnecessarily and passionately enraged at this. We do so many horrible things to each other. But my good friend passively walked away to rest in the hammock, and her calm was remarkable to me for its ease. I know she is not unaware of the things I was saying, but it must be that it no longer weighs on her life. I wish I could find that kind of peace.

For too long we stayed in the Heart of Rocks and immediately upon departure we passed by the Big Balanced Rock for a second time. It's a 1000-ton pillar that has been carved away at the center to create what looks like a dreidel spinning on a stone column. But this time, to get a better look, I walked into the center of the formations to see its silhouette against the sun. And in this moment, I found my sanctuary. The rocks created a large circle around me, near 50-meters in diameter, but each rising almost 50-feet or more into the air. And in the center was only grass, a few shrubs, and I standing there alone. I felt that they were praying over me, and wishing me a safe journey ahead. I was surprised that this spot, not 10-feet off trail, hadn't been named or reserved. But it was probably intentionally so, to keep people out. And it was more magical that way – I felt as if I had opened the doors to a temple, and there in the sunset knew that everything would be all right in the end.

There are places where men don't go, and these places are the last of the cathedrals. Without worrying too much about the world at large, I can go there in good company and find restoration. It is my own prayer and only the rocks are listening. That is something I can believe in.

I Will Not Miss These Things

As you reach the halfway point on the North Franklin Mountain trail, heading southward during an ascent from Mundy's Gap, just as the ridgeline trail meets the summit trail, there looking westward you can see the canyon below and the city further beyond. At your feet there, and for miles in each direction along the eastward side of the summit, is an unexplained number of unexploded ordnances from the years spent blasting rockets, artillery, rifles, missiles, and cannons of all kind into the mountain for testing, or something. You can take the trail up to the summit from this point, but there's only a single trail leading down, a single stretch cleared out of the side of the mountain where otherwise you might find a Vietnam-era mine waiting for you. I know this because there was a day, the second time I tried to summit the north peak, that I reached this area, my furthest point yet. I hadn't really tried to summit the peak before and ran out of daylight each time, but I've never gone past this spot. There's a giant sign in the ground and a long chain of fence keeping the hikers from descending improperly, lest they blow the fuck up. I didn't get higher because I spent maybe thirty to forty minutes staring at it and thinking, what have we done?, or, what hasn't been done to clean it up? and, why not? I lost daylight thinking about it, and I haven't gone back to try the summit again. I will not miss the opportunity for the loss.

I will not miss the mountains, in their empty and uninspiring way, for being so corrupted by the city below. When my wife came back for the second time we had a discussion about this place and what makes it so difficult to breathe. I've been confused for some time why a place that is situated in a river pass between two small mountain ranges could be so filled with grief, and in some time I knew the answer – from any perspective near or far, I couldn't see the mountains for the city below. The first time I drove into the city, the first time I came down from the Sierra Blanca ridge, that day when the sun bore through the clouds and lit the valley below and the sight line stretched for a hundred miles, right there in the middle you could pick out an entire thunderstorm that looked merely cartoonish and singular in the space around it, the rain banding downward like a showerhead and in an hour I'd be covered with rain. Driving in that day I was bewildered at the sight of the mountains. But never since. I remember being equally struck by the endless stream of strip malls and car dealerships and how everything was so colored with the blasting of the sand against the walls of the buildings. It seemed like a suburban sprawl that never started but never ended either. And I will not miss that city below.

The city is among the dirtiest I have known, and not from the sand and rocks and dirt that soak its atmosphere. It is littered with trash. From my porch I can look up the short hill behind the parking lot and see ten twenty thirty bushes with something stuck in it; plastic bags, bottles, potato chip sacks, papers of all kinds. What the wind doesn't blow out, the rest is thrown on the ground by the people of the city. I will not miss the people of this city either.

Driving home there's a new billboard posted. It's in the spot where just after the downtown there are two highways running parallel. Primarily the interstate, but just southward and below is Highway 85. Highway 85 is, for about three miles, the literal border. If you drive southward on Highway 85 from Sunland Park, the concrete shoulder of the highway is the border fence. Well, it is the fence insofar as it has on top of the concrete walls a 10-foot high, 3-foot thick copper and brass fence that even a bird couldn't pass through. This fence starts here and follows the city's line for the populace's entirety, and continues on each direction. In certain high-traffic areas there are two such fences running parallel, a distance of about 100-feet between them. They are lit on all sides by a series of halogen lights, each light pole only 10-feet apart, running for 24-hours-a-day for maximum visibility in all conditions. The border patrol places a manned Chevrolet Tahoe every quarter-mile in these high-traffic areas. They rove the space between, a quarter-mile at a time. And, in what I guess is the most trafficked area, the fence even has inverted lips along the top, sometimes barbed wire. I will not miss the fence.

The effect of the fence, the effect of the people who transition daily from side to side, the final causality of El Paso is that it is stripped of any culture. The displaced people who come here in the military refer to this as Mexico, because it is clearly not Texas. But tellingly, it is neither Mexican. Those who got across at a time when there wasn't a fence and those who come here daily for work or recreation, they come here to get away from Mexico. And they've brought none of it with them. They've replaced whatever culture they had (and wanted to leave behind) with what is the assumed American identity – what we lack for taco trucks, communal and religious events, colorful homes, and tight communities, we make up for in Red Lobsters, Olive Gardens, JC Penney's, PF Chang's, movie theaters, car dealerships, McDonald's, Burger Kings, Starbucks, Whataburgers, shopping malls, Best Buys, Wal-Marts, gas stations, Subways, Taco Bells (no, seriously), Barnes & Nobles (there's only two, but they represent the entirety of booksellers in El Paso), and car washes. I didn't understand at first why there were so many car washes until I spent two weeks here. But more than the dust, I am disgusted by how difficult it is to find a local foodstuff. The best, and really only, genuine burrito I've found comes from a converted gas station by a business founded in Juarez. Its ingredients are all slow-grilled in large vats, and their tortillas are handmade each morning. The place is called Burritos Crisostomo, and it has two locations. Everyone I talk to says it pales in comparison to El Taco Tote. El Taco Tote is an El Paso foundation, and is best compared to a Chipotle, stuffed into a Dairy Queen building. I do not eat at El

Taco Tote. I will not miss El Taco Tote.

Looking for any other kind of independent foodstuff, local or otherwise, can be counted on two hands. There's two pizza places, (Nona's and Ardovino's), an extension of Austin's County Line Barbeque (here called State Line Barbeque), the aforementioned Burritos Crisostomo, Kiki's Mexican (the oldest and most original Mexican restaurant in town that no one goes to), La Malinche (for menudo), and Casa Pizza (which is actually a Greek sandwich shop that makes the best salami subs). This rest is a smattering of corporate foodstuffs that have the longest lines and numerous locations. This wouldn't be surprising if it were a burgeoning frontier township striving for capital growth. But El Paso alone, excluding Juarez, is the country's 14th largest municipality and has nearly a million people. They all eat at Red Lobster.

The reason for this, again, is the desire to seem American. The sad triviality of this is the cyclical and non-expansive nature of El Paso's population. Outsiders do not come here, El Pasoans do not leave. The University of Texas at El Paso boasts a student body over 25,000, but I assure you that most come from the city itself. They graduate and return to the workforce in El Paso as the few who do not labor. Because of this, the education system remains mired in a spiral, teaching its students to grow up and become teachers of future El Paso students, and for their lack of broad and divisive course study, they do not burden their current and future students with any thought of improvement, change, deference. El Paso is as it was and as it will continue to be: a city of poverty, labor, low-income, and poor man's education. It bleeds into every facet of character both visual and visceral and cannot be misunderstood by anyone who spends more than a day here. Because if you spend any time longer than a day, you will see that anything that was sacred in El Paso is no longer. And that can only be allowed by an entirely uneducated population.

There are of course the mountains that will never be

cleared of explosives, but there is also the ghost town comprising El Paso's former downtown. The brochures attempt to sell you on the historic nature of the Plaza Theater, the multiple Kress Buildings once running the famous Kress Department Stores, the Oregon Street shopping district. It is, I say assuredly, a photographer's paradise. The kind of empty, decrepit relics of postwar booming American cities – neon signs that haven't lit in decades, candy-striped barber poles, hand-painted advertisements, handcrafted aluminum signs and banners, individually numbered curbsides, aluminum awnings and full corner glassworks, red brick walls with giant painted Coca-Cola logos. It's the kind of scene straight from Bogdonavich's *The Last Picture Show* and it encompasses every corner of downtown. In one notoriously jaded lower floor, there's a stretch of windows plastered with make-believe images of stores that could be housed in the empty storefronts, emblazed with the words "this store could be you!" I doubt if there's been a store in any of these buildings since the 80s, and I wonder if ever there will be again.

This is remarkable but entirely credible because the city is constructed of a commuter's world. From its westward extremity to its furthest eastward point, El Paso stretches from 36-miles. My own commute to work is 26 miles. It stretches from the west side of the North Franklin peak all the way down to the pass, and then east and southward along the border until just after San Elizario. San Elizario represents the end of the municipality as well as the only remaining bit of culture. San Elizario is famous for being the only jail that Billy The Kid escaped from, which is the dubious variety of fame, but nonetheless. Pat Garrett was here the sheriff, and you know this from the stories. Each of the first Fridays here in San Elizario is an event called Art Fridays where the well-maintained adobe hut buildings that comprise the downtown square open up with art galleries, wine, sidewalk projection shows, and live music. The only people who go are the ones who operate the event. The other 900,000 people all miss it, and I will not miss them.

Because everyday I drive home and one of these 900,000 people nearly take my life on the highway. Driving home is a dangerous activity here. If not for the poorly constructed weave of highways, or the central traffic funneling that is the interstate, or the endless construction zones throughout the city, then mostly for the people using the roads. A few bad drivers are blemishes to the record, but a city that experiences a dozen wrecks in a single rush hour has an endemic problem. This, the traffic and its inefficacy, is the largest and singular proof of the city's problems and cultural clashes. Because there are two types of people on the roads here, split in unequal numbers; there are the native, uneducated poor who drive well below the speed limit from what I assume is a great fear of death, police involvement, and a cost they cannot afford, and there is the non-native, uneducated poor in the military who through ignorance treat the world like a playground and only drive as fast as possible. There are no less than 10 cars abandoned on the side of the highway during my commute, every day. There are no less than 1-in-10 cars driving on spare tires. This is a big one for me, because it is the sad evidence of two terrible ways of life: the first, that the driver got in some accident to lose a tire; the second, that they have not the income or budget skills to replace the spare. The types of vehicles that make up the roads are the types of vehicle that you sold to a dealership ten years ago. Here there are ten trucks for every car, and not because we need trucks in El Paso. El Pasoans drive trucks because they are old, cheap, and can be purchased easily. When it breaks down, I assume they replace it with another 1997 Dodge Ram, as most have and are. Just the other day I tried to park in the garage of the University Medical Center, but it took fifteen minutes just to navigate to the fourth floor, because the trucks trying to drive and park in there were too big and driven by people who couldn't handle the size of a 2500 series hauling truck. It's not because they need a truck –

it's because they need a vehicle they can purchase in cash, in whole, and for cheap. That vehicle will be driven until it cannot, and then it will be replaced. Whether by falling behind on maintenance or by totaling the truck in a wreck doesn't matter.

And they wreck so frequently. Often, and by my own experience driving in Europe, I've learned that we teach our drivers in America to drive defensively to a fault, instead of driving aggressively. The intent of the adjective *aggressive* is not to provoke stupidity, but to instigate vigilance – the vigilance to be aware and cognizant of a vehicle's surroundings. But by fearing aggressive driving for misunderstanding it as *fast* and *dangerous*, we default to defensive driving for sake of *safety* and *isolation* from fault. The thinking goes that, "if I don't do anything wrong, nothing can happen to me." This is manifested mostly in the failure to obey any right-of-way or fast-lane designations, and primarily occurs in wrecks where entrance ramps enter the highway. Never once does a vehicle on the highway allow another vehicle to enter. To compound the situation, the vehicles entering the highway often *decelerate out of fear* to find an open space, rather than accelerate. And in the many cases where this results in a wreck, the immediate response is a shaking motion of the hands and the phrase "no police, no police." I've seen this many times, and expect it many times more. But it is not their fault for fearing the police. It is our fault for creating this place. It is our fault for putting up a fence, divesting half the workforce, separating families, stifling the already poor, and enforcing it through fear. It is our fault for creating a world that has yet to open its boundaries. It is our fault for being patriotic to a written document instead of to the human race. It is our fault for filling this city with problems and leaving it to rot. I will not miss the rot.

This city came to these problems the same way any other has. But only because it started in the muck, it buries itself even further with the added contemporary problems of a mortgage-crisis, low-unemployment, and border security. There is here, like there is in all the world, a growing population driven by consumer interest. But where a city like New York or Tokyo or Paris might have the standard quality of life to allow its citizens the luxury of a new smartphone, El Paso cripples itself by choosing to buy the latest smartphone even when household income cannot support it. At every stoplight, the lead car is slow to accelerate because the driver is staring downward into a smartphone. This is not an exaggeration. It is doubly worse on Fort Bliss. Without failure, every car that I see swerving and driving with inconsistent speed is driven by a person that is looking at a smartphone. Just last week it was only my horn-honking that saved the Jeep in front of me from smashing into the highway barrier instead of curving with the road. It wouldn't be so endemically true except that the places of highest congestion occur where there are shopping malls. I live near one. On every weekend, the roads there back up through all intersections. These people do not go hiking, do not go downtown, do not go out, they only go shopping. They spend what little money they have on things, just things, and do nothing to improve their way of life. The city's parks are not parks, they are dead-grass fields with a few lights. There is no entertainment in El Paso because the people wouldn't go. There are no arts districts, there are no independent shops or bakeries or clothing stores, there are no live events. There are only shopping malls. I will not miss the shopping malls.

It is not their fault. We have created an education system that teaches us to want things, and to work for the money to have things. We do not teach our children to work for ideas or fulfillment. We do not teach them to work for life-enriching experiences, nor emotional stability. We teach them to work for money, and money buys things. Our status and fulfillment is derived from our possessions, our visual manifestation of who-we-are-*vis-a-vis*-what-we-have. This is a problem everywhere, but it is a depressing reality in a city that should not afford its luxury. This is a city that should be building and cleaning and developing a better future. This is a future full of people that wanted to be better, but they stopped improving just after crossing the fence. We've taught people on both sides of the fence that over here it's better because we have *things*, and access to *things*. "If only we could get the things, our life would be better." And the people already on this side of the fence, we won't let them over anymore to take the *things* we already possess. But we have so little things, and each of them are unimportant. If the people here could understand that. If only they could see all the *things* blowing here in the wind, the *things* littering the sides of the road, filling up the trash containers, and sitting around wasting in the desert sun. These were things that were bought on Saturday but were useless by Monday, and thrown out. Not thrown anywhere particular, just out. Out onto the ground, into the desert, out of the room and no longer a problem. There is a special kind of laziness that only a poor education can create that allows this type of ignorance, this deference to nature and humanity both. It is an education derived of living for, possessing, and needing *things*.

Things. They are just *things*. I will not miss the *things*.

The same education that made this possible made the war that made the job I have possible. But this education infects the other 400-million people of this country as well. I will not miss serving in this capacity. It worked for me insofar as its benefits to my own life outweighed the negative effects incurred. For so long as it paid me a substantial amount to erase my student loan debt, I could suffer it. For so long as it subsidized my life in Europe, I could suffer it. For so long as it emboldened my experiences and placed me within an environment of curiosity and wonder, I could suffer it. But it does none of these things any longer, and I will not miss it. I will not miss the city that it brought me to, or the people that continue to suffer it. I will not miss the handshakes I receive for defending a country that shouldn't be defended, and I will not miss the uniform that places me within a peculiar and isolated portion of society. I have done good things while in the military, but many of them are a result ancillary. The places I have gone, the things I have learned, the people I have met and the women I have loved, these are all indirect benefits of a system that now exists only to ruin my mind and further my depression, and I will not miss it.

I will not miss filling my days with data and facts and figures that amount to war. I will not miss knowing that my work, when even its fullest contribution and development still only totals about one-four-hundred-thousandth of the Army's power and capability, comprises that small amount of this nation's power for war. I will not miss hearing phrases like "combat power" and "force strength" and "shoot, maneuver, kill" and "strike the enemy" at simple board meetings and welcoming conferences, as if these phrases were as common as "brand synergy" and "competitive value" and "marketing power." I will not miss being told to "impact soldiers" when there is no way for me to have an impact – if I present myself wholly, truly, and genuinely for the person I am, I am met with derision; I am not like these people - I read, I wonder, I think, I believe in peace, and I speak clearly. In order to make an impact, to have influence, I have to become, and have become, one of them. I will not miss being one of them. I miss being inspired, I miss being creative, I miss believing that everything is possible. And to get that back I have to be free of this, and I've errantly found a way. As has happened numerous times before, I've found another way to return to nature, return to searching, return to freshness. I've found another way to screw up, and I miss the feeling it gives me. I can do anything again. The end is here, but the beginning is coming up right behind.

No matter how the end comes, it is here and I will not miss it. Everyone I know repeats the same phrase unprovoked – I never belonged in the Army. I contend that there were moments when I did belong. There were moments, moments sitting along the Salzach river or the Italian beaches of Porto

Ferro, moments drinking oak-barrel scotch from the frozen Finnish pubs, moments sipping mulled-wine next to a fire on Christmas listening to the village folk band play traditional hymns in a 10-piece brass band, moments when listening to my new Czech friends DJ their latest set at an underground club in Prague, moments running from the bulls in Spain, moments lying in the snow of the rolling farmlands of the German hinterland, moments when I felt at home that I could belong in the Army. In those moments I belonged, even though the Army made those moments possible. But it no longer makes those moments possible and I am irreparably depressed for it, and I will not miss it.

The strongest, most lasting thing I learned is that I have lived overseas, and it is not so hard to do again. It seemed so foreign when I did it the first time, but I've physically done it now – I can physically do it again. The means are not important because I have the desire, the will, and the knowledge now. It is a skill gained, like any other skill of boot-crafting, sport, musical, or otherwise. It's been done, and I know a little bit now of how to do it again. If everyone could get this just once, they might do it again. But until then, they are doomed to comfort and security. Doomed to a home in one place. But the world is one place. The earth is one home.

I was pilfering through old photos an old friend of mine had posted online, a good large collection of pictures of people I grew up with and all the things they had done. I remember all of these moments too, days in junior high and days in high school, in and around my hometown. All the people I had grown up with in a small town where everyone knew everyone, all the people were there. There were the heartbreaking photos of the many friends I had that are now deceased, the moments we shared. There were poor fashion choices and high school pep rallies and pictures taken during an innocuous lunch on a random school-day afternoon. In each of these moments were precious memories, but I wasn't in a single photograph. I wasn't snapped or taken or involved. If I asked this person or these people to recount the details of our collective childhood, I have a place in all of them, and yet I'm not represented in the pictographic evidence even once. I was always there for everyone, always on the border, but never really inside these circles.

I always felt like I didn't belong or wouldn't get in with these people, and I can remember a lot of these moments exactly as I'm viewing them now in the pictures – from just out of frame. There, but not really. And I wonder why, until I realize that it wasn't that I didn't belong. I just didn't get in there.

I didn't really care to get in there. I think I have this shared, collective experience with almost everyone I have ever known. The geeks, the band nerds, the athletes, the popular kids, the outcasts. Everyone called me a friend, but I'm not a part of any one's most cherished memory. When everyone cut their hair, I grew mine out. When everyone wore polo shirts and stripes, I wore tees and solid colors. When everyone listened to hip-hop I went to the rock'n'roll show. I did it on purpose because I didn't want to fit in. I relished it, even when I thought it would help me get along. But I know now that what I truly wanted was to be different. I know this now.

I don't know if I'll ever find a group, and I probably won't. My beliefs have always been too broad, too strong, too universal, too enriched and empowering. The kinds of beliefs that others find offensive because it belittles their insignificant problems and worries for not being larger, more abstract, and unable to hold or make sense of. Unimportant.

What's important is that I need to stop trying to belong. I've forgotten how to not belong.